SO-AKQ-355

STONE ARCH BOOKS
a capstone imprint

STONE ARCH BOOKS™

Published in 2015
by Stone Arch Books
A Capstone Imprint
1710 Roe Crest Drive
North Mankato, MN 56003
www.capstonepub.com

Originally published by DC Comics in
the U.S. in single magazine form as Beware
the Batman #1. Copyright © 2015 DC Comics.
All Rights Reserved.

DC Comics
1700 Broadway, New York, NY 10019
A Warner Bros. Entertainment Company

Cataloging-in-Publication Data is available
at the Library of Congress website:
ISBN: 978-1-4342-9738-9 (library binding)

Summary: Anarky has struck the city of
Gotham, but Bruce Wayne and his team have
discovered the villain's plan: rid Gotham City
of its laws and regulations, and let anarchy
reign! But with a little help from the people
of Gotham, Anarky could lose his chance to let
chaos rule.

STONE ARCH BOOKS
Ashley C. Andersen Zantop *Publisher*
Michael Dahl *Editorial Director*
Sean Tulien *Editor*
Heather Kindseth *Creative Director*
Alison Thiele and Peggie Carley *Designers*
Tori Abraham *Production Specialist*

DC COMICS
Kristy Quinn *Original U.S. Editor*

Printed in China by Nordica.
0914/CA21401510
092014 008470NORD515

BEWARE THE BATMAN™

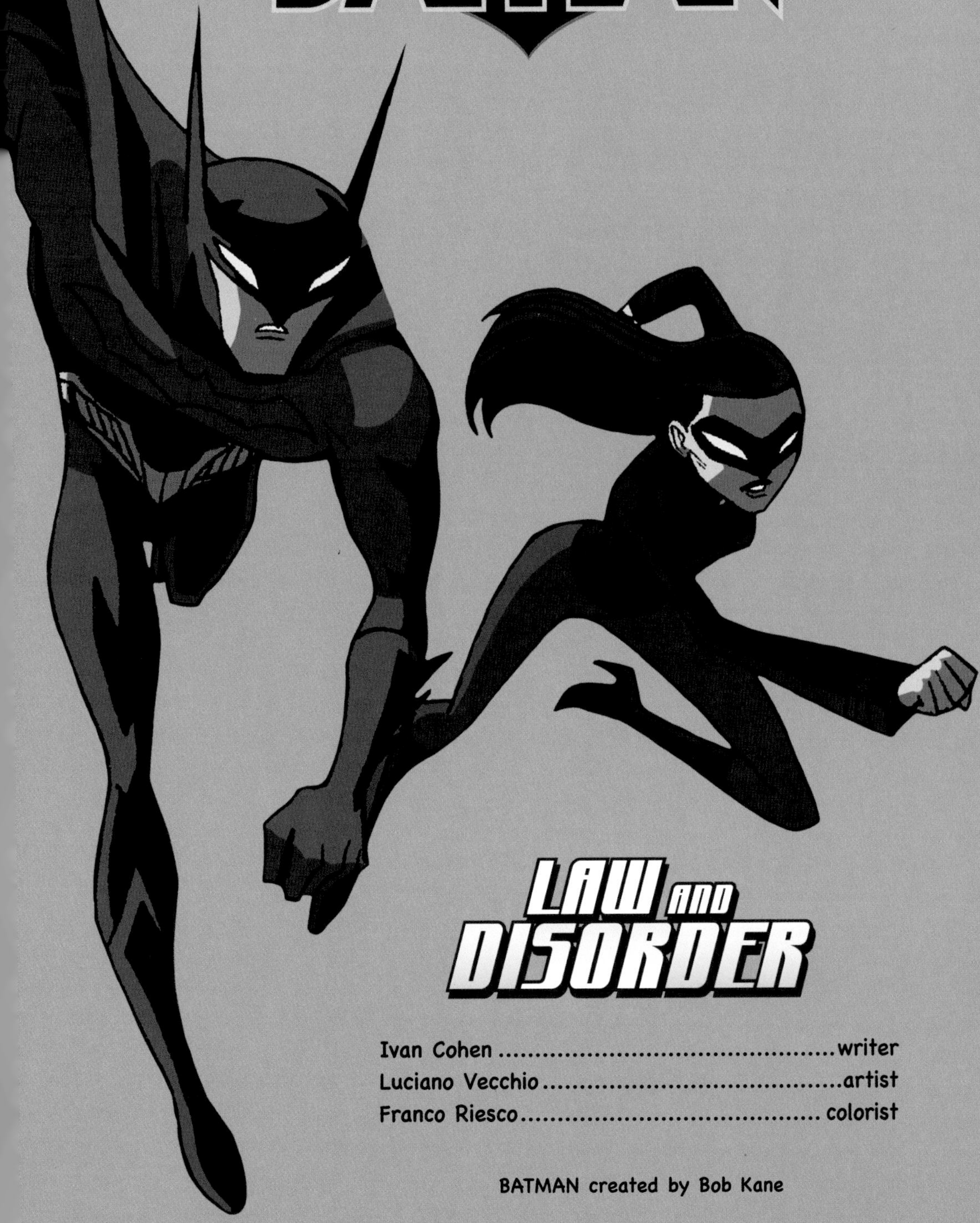

LAW AND DISORDER

Ivan Cohen .... writer
Luciano Vecchio .... artist
Franco Riesco .... colorist

BATMAN created by Bob Kane

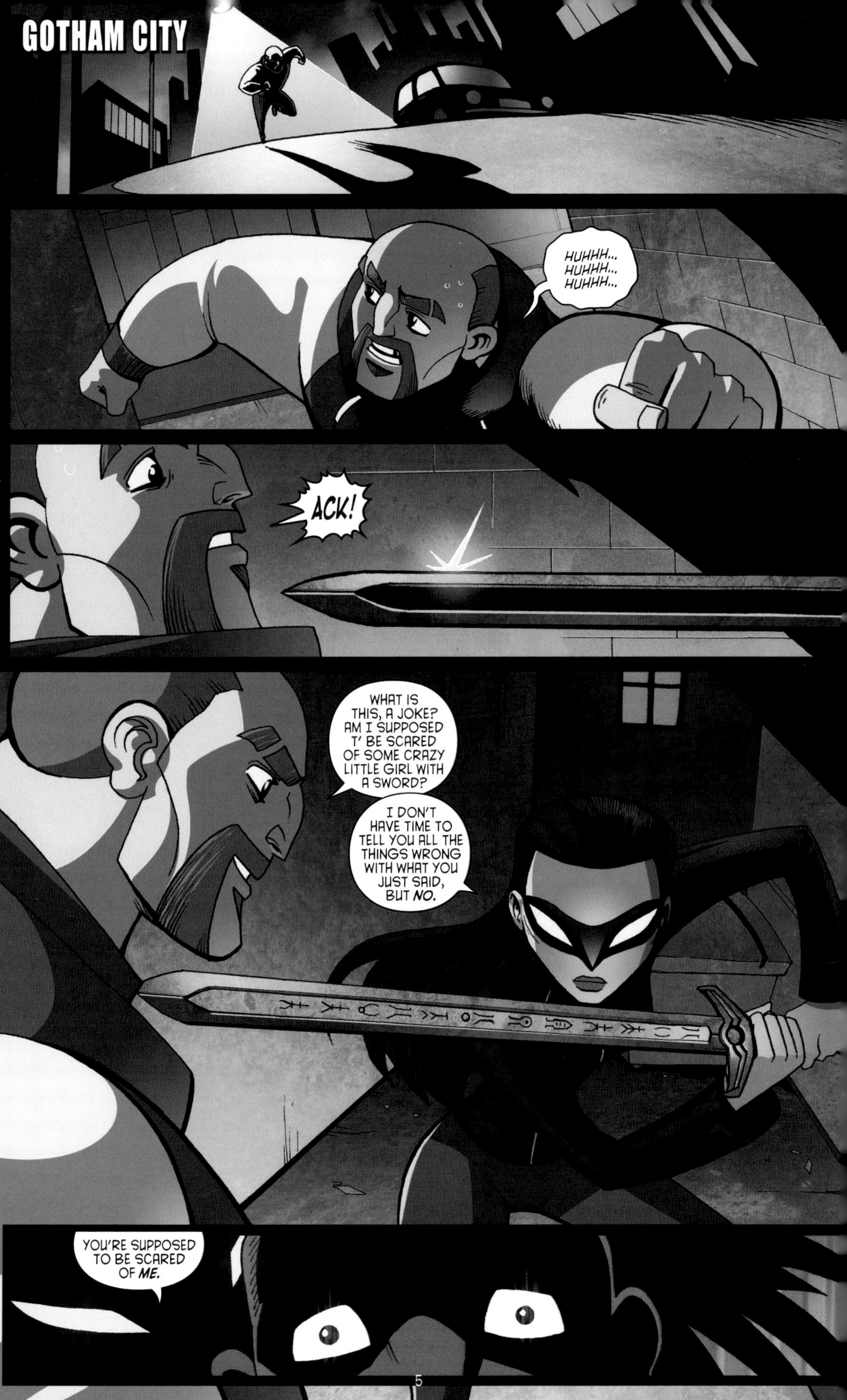
GOTHAM CITY
HUHHH... HUHHH... HUHHH...
ACK!
WHAT IS THIS, A JOKE? AM I SUPPOSED T' BE SCARED OF SOME CRAZY LITTLE GIRL WITH A SWORD?
I DON'T HAVE TIME TO TELL YOU ALL THE THINGS WRONG WITH WHAT YOU JUST SAID, BUT NO.
YOU'RE SUPPOSED TO BE SCARED OF ME.

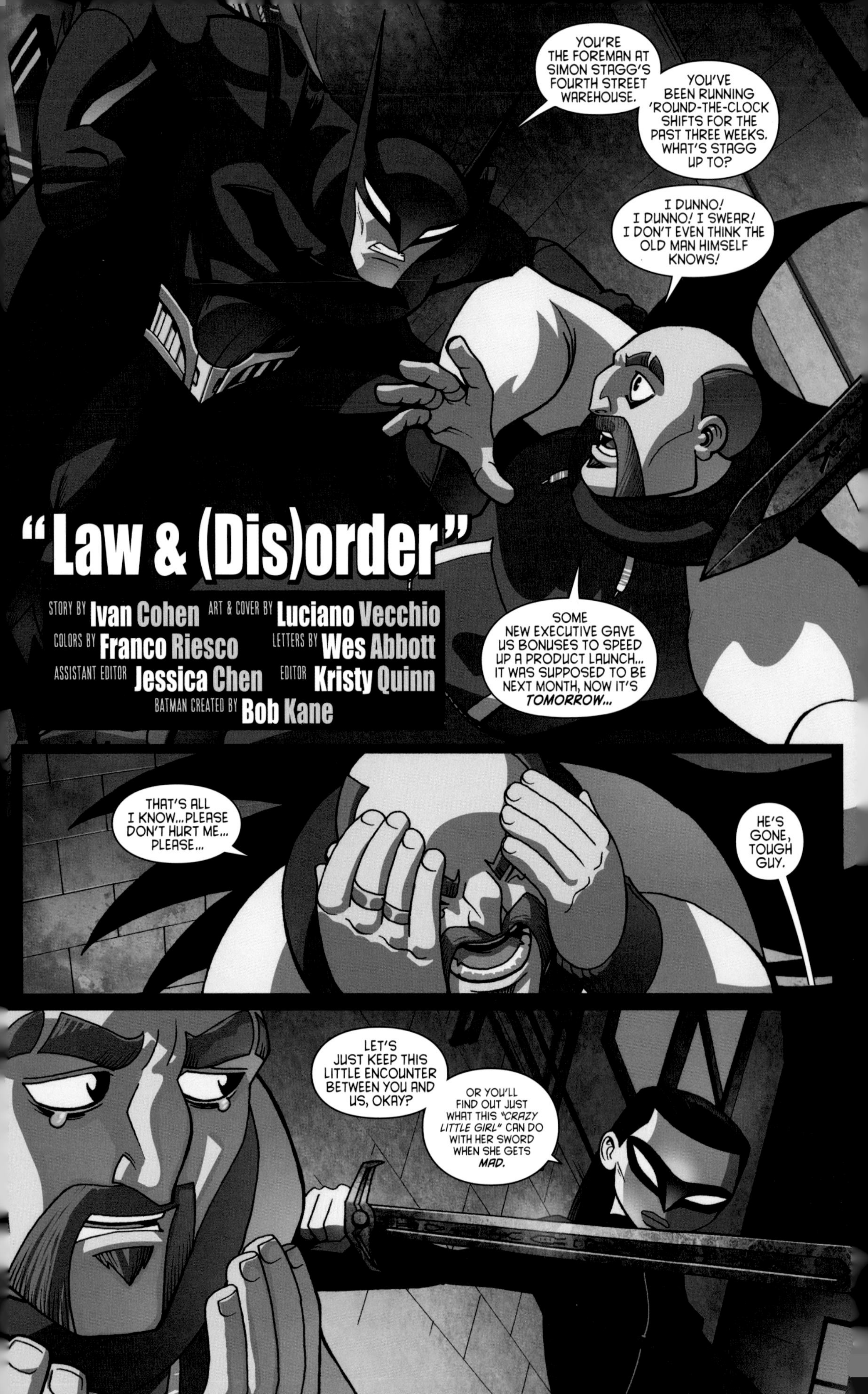
YOU'RE THE FOREMAN AT SIMON STAGG'S FOURTH STREET WAREHOUSE.
YOU'VE BEEN RUNNING 'ROUND-THE-CLOCK SHIFTS FOR THE PAST THREE WEEKS. WHAT'S STAGG UP TO?
I DUNNO! I DUNNO! I SWEAR! I DON'T EVEN THINK THE OLD MAN HIMSELF KNOWS!
"Law & (Dis)order"
STORY BY Ivan Cohen ART & COVER BY Luciano Vecchio
COLORS BY Franco Riesco LETTERS BY Wes Abbott
ASSISTANT EDITOR Jessica Chen EDITOR Kristy Quinn
BATMAN CREATED BY Bob Kane
SOME NEW EXECUTIVE GAVE US BONUSES TO SPEED UP A PRODUCT LAUNCH... IT WAS SUPPOSED TO BE NEXT MONTH, NOW IT'S *TOMORROW...*
THAT'S ALL I KNOW...PLEASE DON'T HURT ME... PLEASE...
HE'S GONE, TOUGH GUY.
LET'S JUST KEEP THIS LITTLE ENCOUNTER BETWEEN YOU AND US, OKAY?
OR YOU'LL FIND OUT JUST WHAT THIS *"CRAZY LITTLE GIRL"* CAN DO WITH HER SWORD WHEN SHE GETS *MAD.*

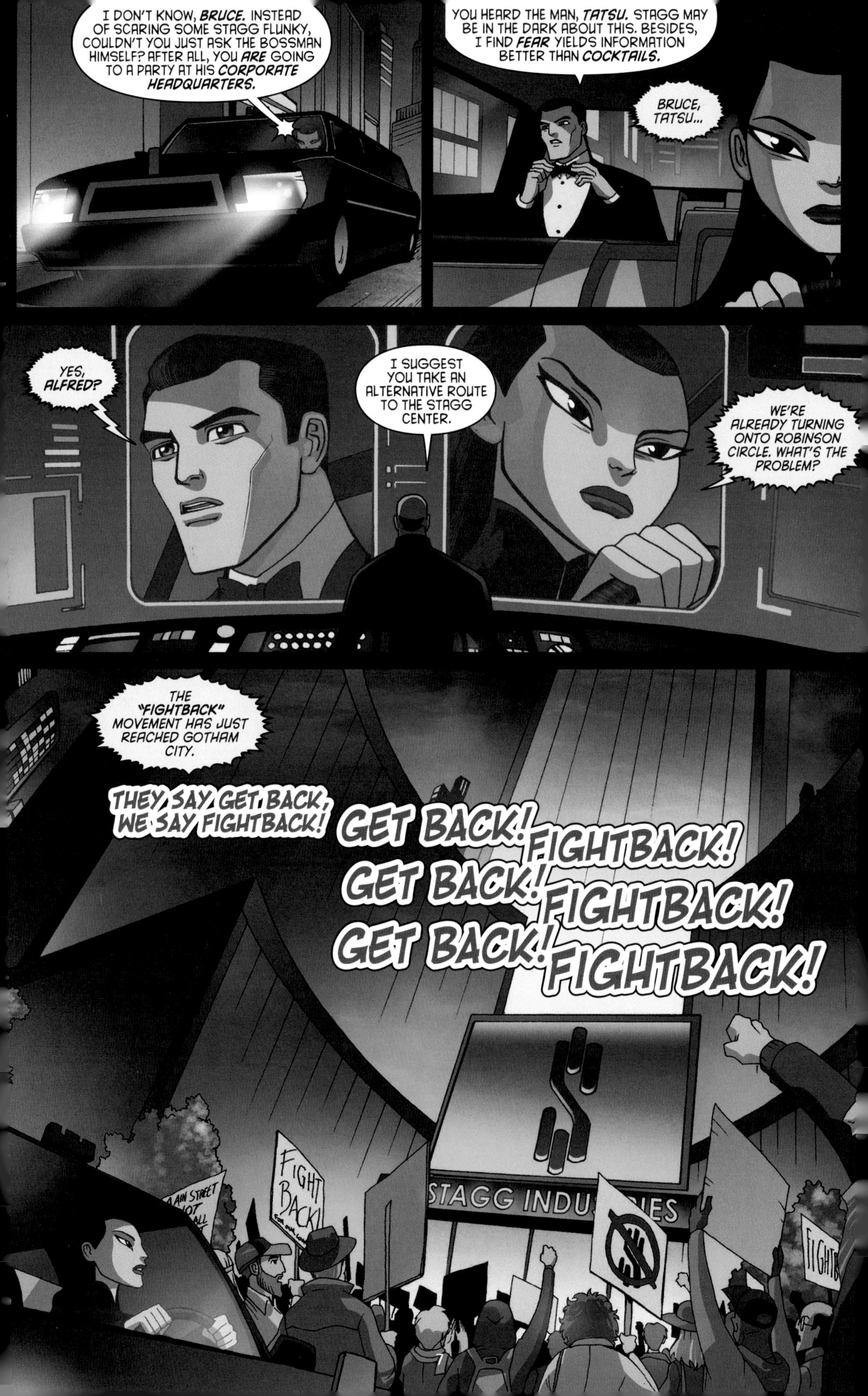
I DON'T KNOW, BRUCE. INSTEAD OF SCARING SOME STAGG FLUNKY, COULDN'T YOU JUST ASK THE BOSSMAN HIMSELF? AFTER ALL, YOU ARE GOING TO A PARTY AT HIS CORPORATE HEADQUARTERS.
YOU HEARD THE MAN, TATSU. STAGG MAY BE IN THE DARK ABOUT THIS. BESIDES, I FIND FEAR YIELDS INFORMATION BETTER THAN COCKTAILS.
BRUCE, TATSU...
YES, ALFRED?
I SUGGEST YOU TAKE AN ALTERNATIVE ROUTE TO THE STAGG CENTER.
WE'RE ALREADY TURNING ONTO ROBINSON CIRCLE. WHAT'S THE PROBLEM?
THE "FIGHTBACK" MOVEMENT HAS JUST REACHED GOTHAM CITY.
THEY SAY GET BACK, WE SAY FIGHTBACK!
GET BACK! FIGHTBACK!
GET BACK! FIGHTBACK!
GET BACK! FIGHTBACK!
FIGHT BACK!

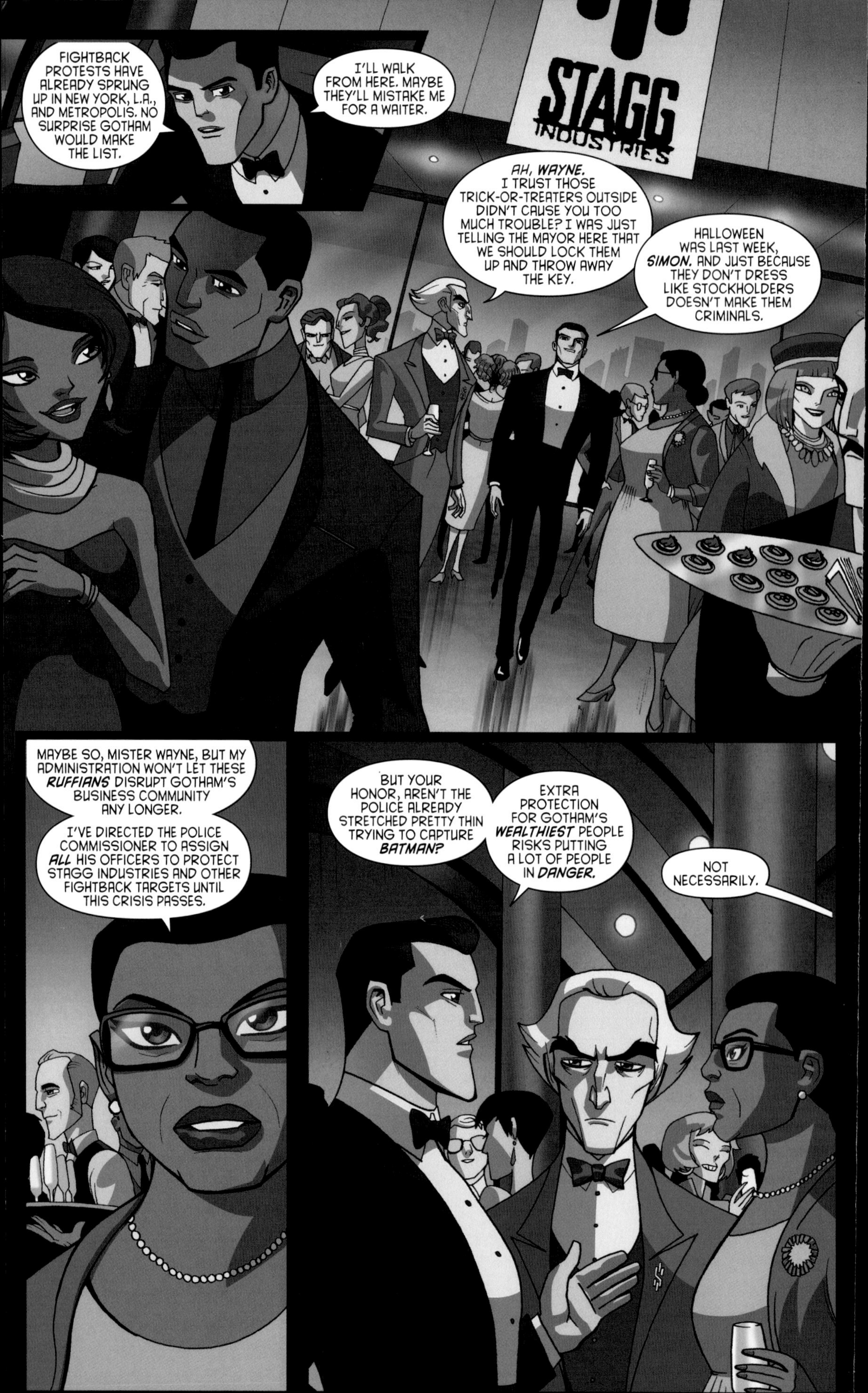
FIGHTBACK PROTESTS HAVE ALREADY SPRUNG UP IN NEW YORK, L.A., AND METROPOLIS. NO SURPRISE GOTHAM WOULD MAKE THE LIST.
I'LL WALK FROM HERE. MAYBE THEY'LL MISTAKE ME FOR A WAITER.
STAGG INDUSTRIES
AH, WAYNE. I TRUST THOSE TRICK-OR-TREATERS OUTSIDE DIDN'T CAUSE YOU TOO MUCH TROUBLE? I WAS JUST TELLING THE MAYOR HERE THAT WE SHOULD LOCK THEM UP AND THROW AWAY THE KEY.
HALLOWEEN WAS LAST WEEK, SIMON. AND JUST BECAUSE THEY DON'T DRESS LIKE STOCKHOLDERS DOESN'T MAKE THEM CRIMINALS.
MAYBE SO, MISTER WAYNE, BUT MY ADMINISTRATION WON'T LET THESE RUFFIANS DISRUPT GOTHAM'S BUSINESS COMMUNITY ANY LONGER.
I'VE DIRECTED THE POLICE COMMISSIONER TO ASSIGN ALL HIS OFFICERS TO PROTECT STAGG INDUSTRIES AND OTHER FIGHTBACK TARGETS UNTIL THIS CRISIS PASSES.
BUT YOUR HONOR, AREN'T THE POLICE ALREADY STRETCHED PRETTY THIN TRYING TO CAPTURE BATMAN?
EXTRA PROTECTION FOR GOTHAM'S WEALTHIEST PEOPLE RISKS PUTTING A LOT OF PEOPLE IN DANGER.
NOT NECESSARILY.

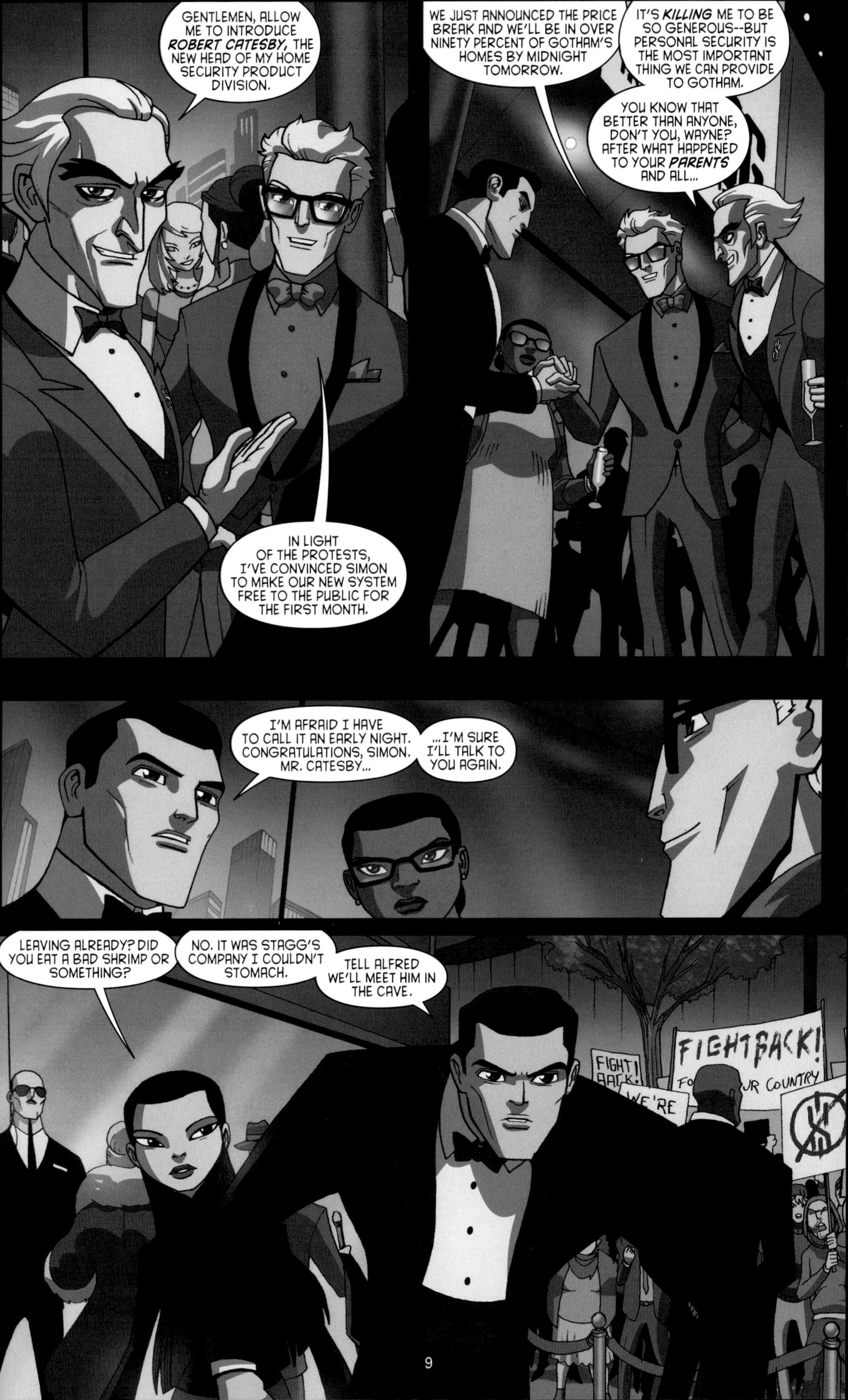
GENTLEMEN, ALLOW ME TO INTRODUCE ROBERT CATESBY, THE NEW HEAD OF MY HOME SECURITY PRODUCT DIVISION.
IN LIGHT OF THE PROTESTS, I'VE CONVINCED SIMON TO MAKE OUR NEW SYSTEM FREE TO THE PUBLIC FOR THE FIRST MONTH.
WE JUST ANNOUNCED THE PRICE BREAK AND WE'LL BE IN OVER NINETY PERCENT OF GOTHAM'S HOMES BY MIDNIGHT TOMORROW.
IT'S KILLING ME TO BE SO GENEROUS--BUT PERSONAL SECURITY IS THE MOST IMPORTANT THING WE CAN PROVIDE TO GOTHAM.
YOU KNOW THAT BETTER THAN ANYONE, DON'T YOU, WAYNE? AFTER WHAT HAPPENED TO YOUR PARENTS AND ALL...
I'M AFRAID I HAVE TO CALL IT AN EARLY NIGHT. CONGRATULATIONS, SIMON. MR. CATESBY...
...I'M SURE I'LL TALK TO YOU AGAIN.
LEAVING ALREADY? DID YOU EAT A BAD SHRIMP OR SOMETHING?
NO. IT WAS STAGG'S COMPANY I COULDN'T STOMACH.
TELL ALFRED WE'LL MEET HIM IN THE CAVE.
FIGHTBACK!
WE'RE

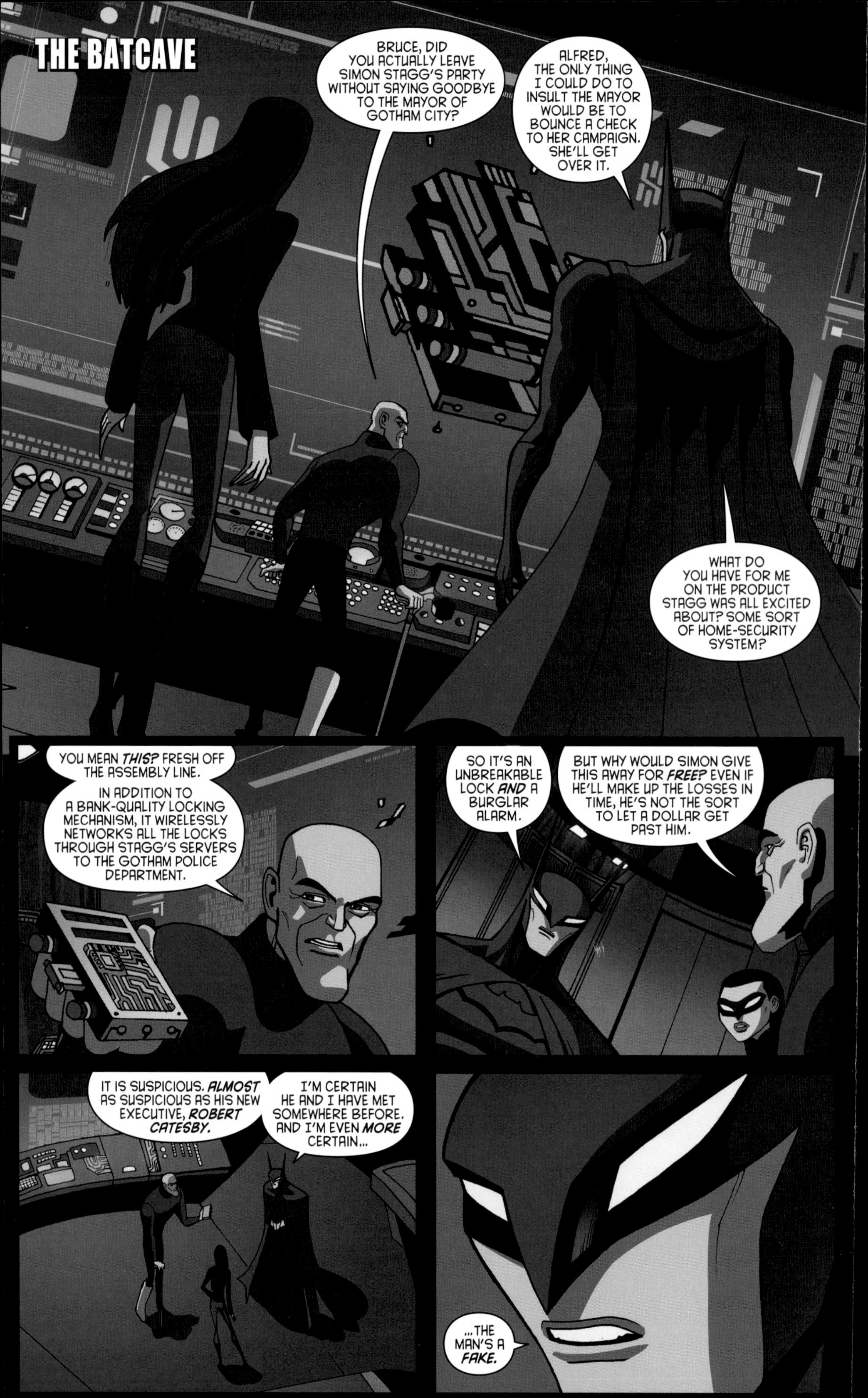
THE BATCAVE
BRUCE, DID YOU ACTUALLY LEAVE SIMON STAGG'S PARTY WITHOUT SAYING GOODBYE TO THE MAYOR OF GOTHAM CITY?
ALFRED, THE ONLY THING I COULD DO TO INSULT THE MAYOR WOULD BE TO BOUNCE A CHECK TO HER CAMPAIGN. SHE'LL GET OVER IT.
WHAT DO YOU HAVE FOR ME ON THE PRODUCT STAGG WAS ALL EXCITED ABOUT? SOME SORT OF HOME-SECURITY SYSTEM?
YOU MEAN *THIS?* FRESH OFF THE ASSEMBLY LINE.
IN ADDITION TO A BANK-QUALITY LOCKING MECHANISM, IT WIRELESSLY NETWORKS ALL THE LOCKS THROUGH STAGG'S SERVERS TO THE GOTHAM POLICE DEPARTMENT.
SO IT'S AN UNBREAKABLE LOCK *AND* A BURGLAR ALARM.
BUT WHY WOULD SIMON GIVE THIS AWAY FOR *FREE?* EVEN IF HE'LL MAKE UP THE LOSSES IN TIME, HE'S NOT THE SORT TO LET A DOLLAR GET PAST HIM.
IT IS SUSPICIOUS. *ALMOST* AS SUSPICIOUS AS HIS NEW EXECUTIVE, *ROBERT CATESBY.*
I'M CERTAIN HE AND I HAVE MET SOMEWHERE BEFORE. AND I'M EVEN *MORE* CERTAIN...
...THE MAN'S A *FAKE.*

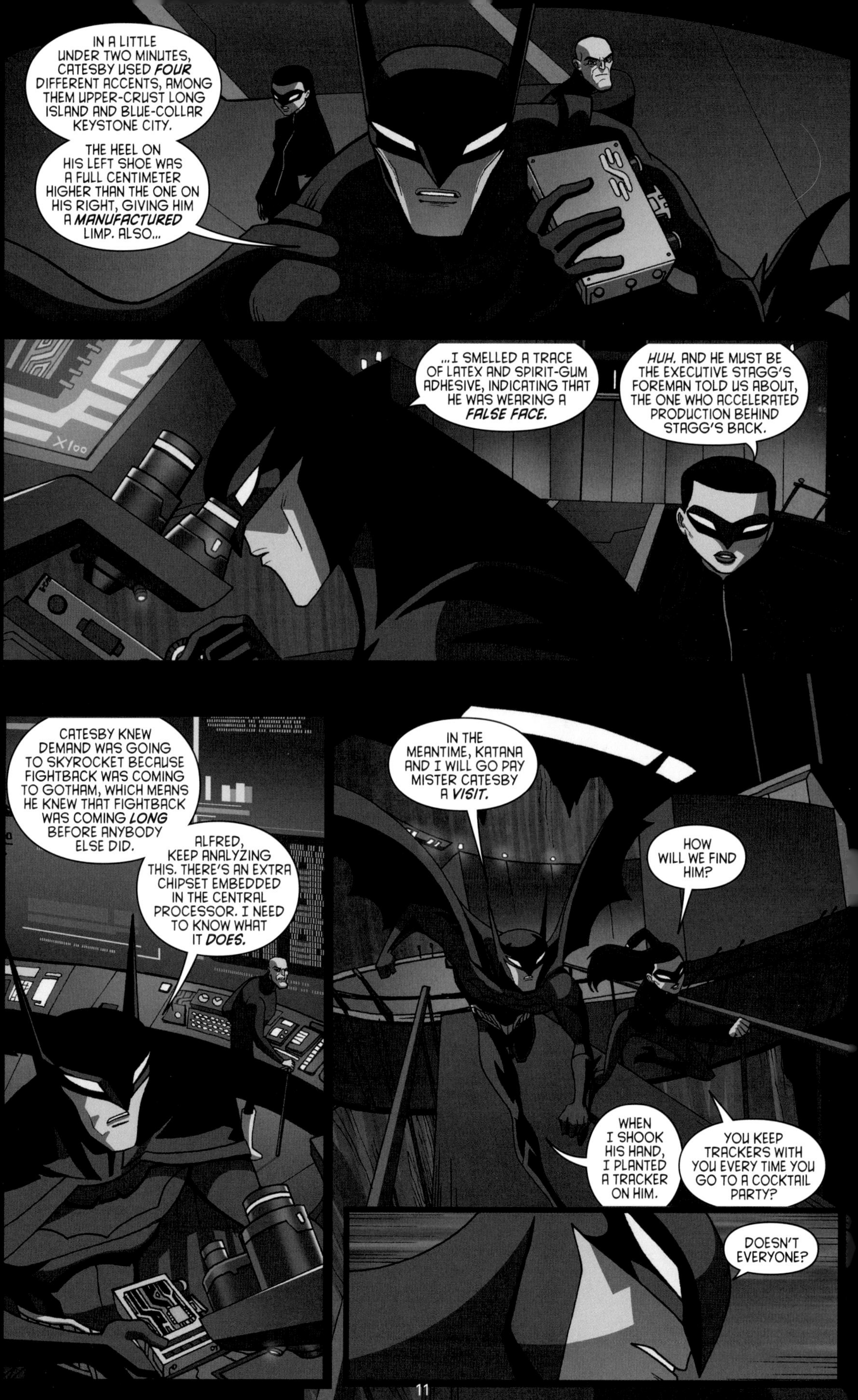
IN A LITTLE UNDER TWO MINUTES, CATESBY USED FOUR DIFFERENT ACCENTS, AMONG THEM UPPER-CRUST LONG ISLAND AND BLUE-COLLAR KEYSTONE CITY.
THE HEEL ON HIS LEFT SHOE WAS A FULL CENTIMETER HIGHER THAN THE ONE ON HIS RIGHT, GIVING HIM A MANUFACTURED LIMP. ALSO...
...I SMELLED A TRACE OF LATEX AND SPIRIT-GUM ADHESIVE, INDICATING THAT HE WAS WEARING A FALSE FACE.
HUH. AND HE MUST BE THE EXECUTIVE STAGG'S FOREMAN TOLD US ABOUT, THE ONE WHO ACCELERATED PRODUCTION BEHIND STAGG'S BACK.
CATESBY KNEW DEMAND WAS GOING TO SKYROCKET BECAUSE FIGHTBACK WAS COMING TO GOTHAM, WHICH MEANS HE KNEW THAT FIGHTBACK WAS COMING LONG BEFORE ANYBODY ELSE DID.
ALFRED, KEEP ANALYZING THIS. THERE'S AN EXTRA CHIPSET EMBEDDED IN THE CENTRAL PROCESSOR. I NEED TO KNOW WHAT IT DOES.
IN THE MEANTIME, KATANA AND I WILL GO PAY MISTER CATESBY A VISIT.
HOW WILL WE FIND HIM?
WHEN I SHOOK HIS HAND, I PLANTED A TRACKER ON HIM.
YOU KEEP TRACKERS WITH YOU EVERY TIME YOU GO TO A COCKTAIL PARTY?
DOESN'T EVERYONE?

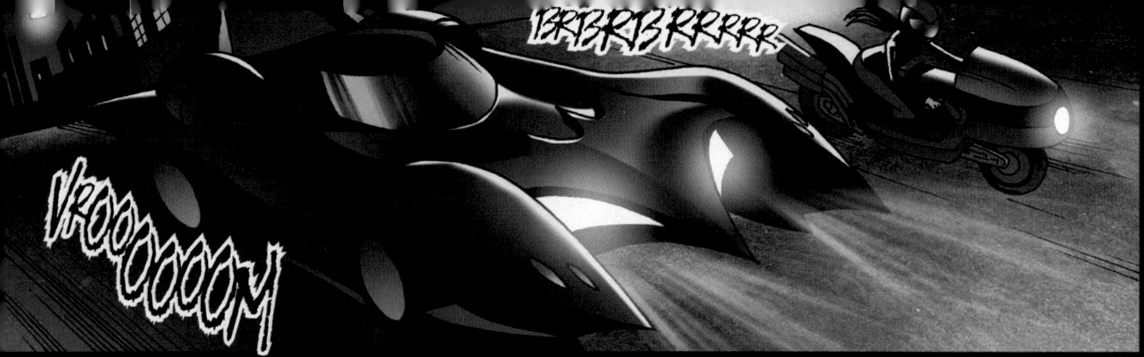
BRBRBRRRRR
VROOOOOOM

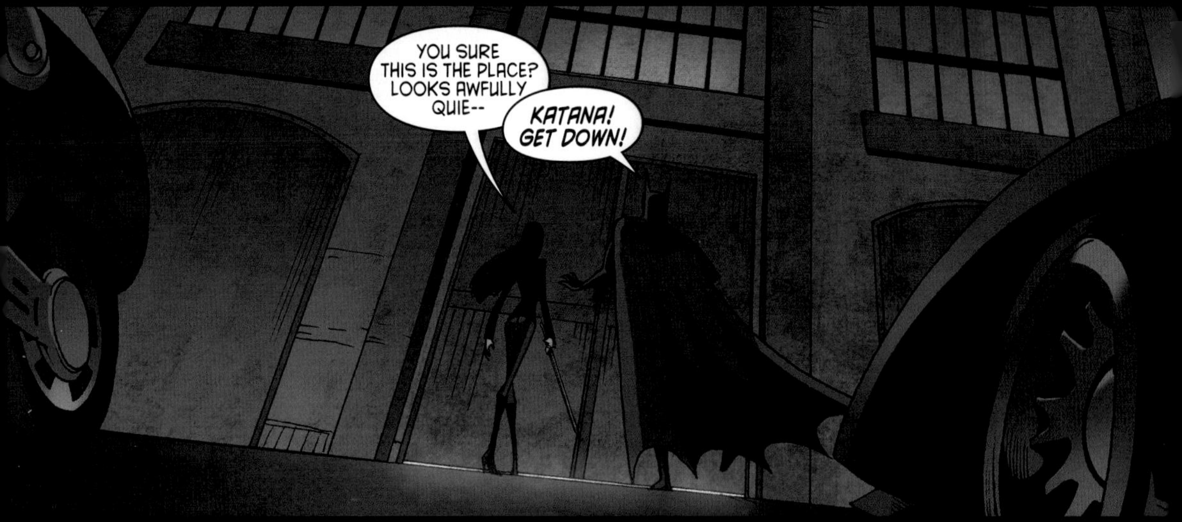
YOU SURE THIS IS THE PLACE? LOOKS AWFULLY QUIE--
KATANA! GET DOWN!

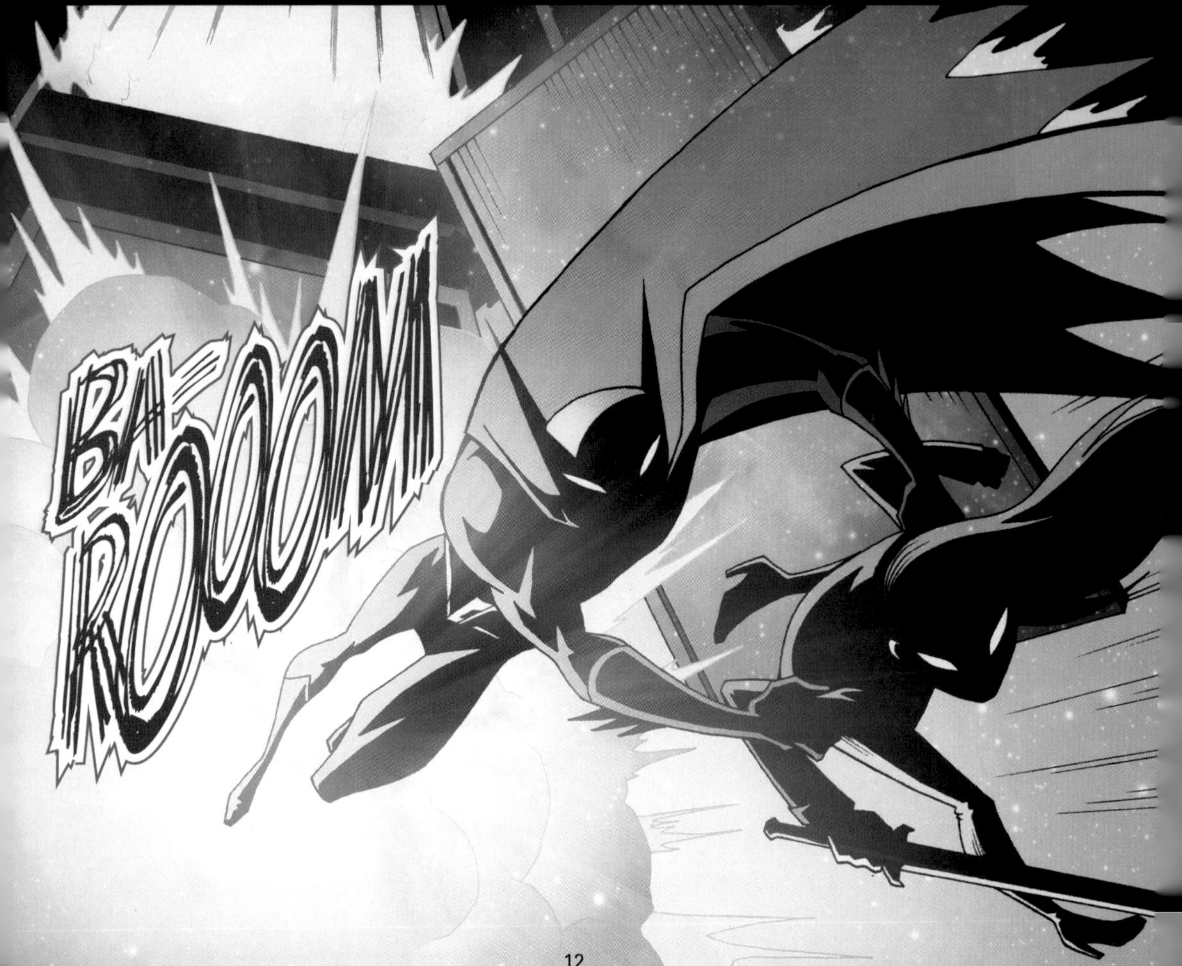
BA-ROOOOM

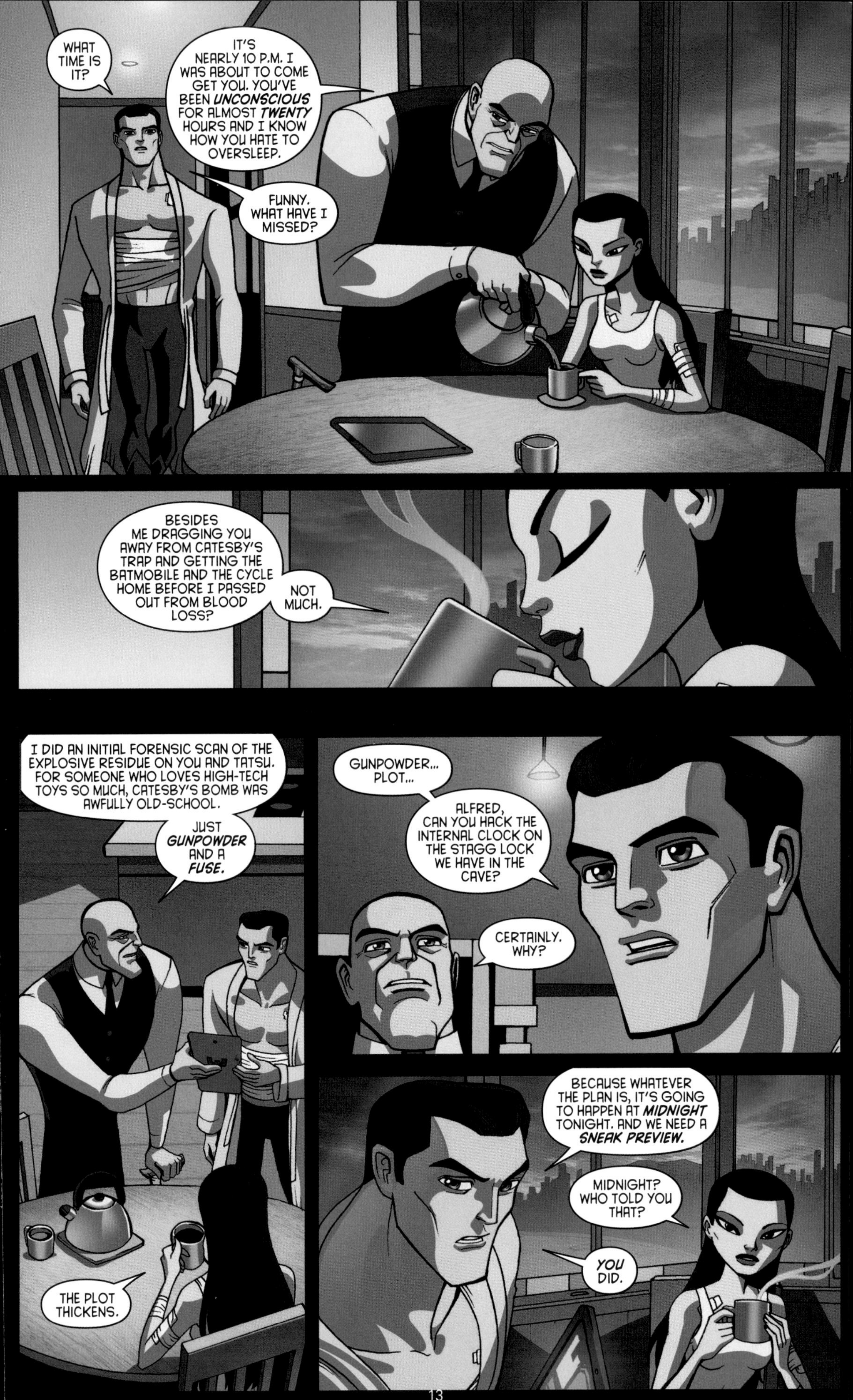
WHAT TIME IS IT?
IT'S NEARLY 10 P.M. I WAS ABOUT TO COME GET YOU. YOU'VE BEEN UNCONSCIOUS FOR ALMOST TWENTY HOURS AND I KNOW HOW YOU HATE TO OVERSLEEP.
FUNNY. WHAT HAVE I MISSED?
BESIDES ME DRAGGING YOU AWAY FROM CATESBY'S TRAP AND GETTING THE BATMOBILE AND THE CYCLE HOME BEFORE I PASSED OUT FROM BLOOD LOSS?
NOT MUCH.
I DID AN INITIAL FORENSIC SCAN OF THE EXPLOSIVE RESIDUE ON YOU AND TATSU. FOR SOMEONE WHO LOVES HIGH-TECH TOYS SO MUCH, CATESBY'S BOMB WAS AWFULLY OLD-SCHOOL.
JUST GUNPOWDER AND A FUSE.
THE PLOT THICKENS.
GUNPOWDER... PLOT...
ALFRED, CAN YOU HACK THE INTERNAL CLOCK ON THE STAGG LOCK WE HAVE IN THE CAVE?
CERTAINLY. WHY?
BECAUSE WHATEVER THE PLAN IS, IT'S GOING TO HAPPEN AT MIDNIGHT TONIGHT. AND WE NEED A SNEAK PREVIEW.
MIDNIGHT? WHO TOLD YOU THAT?
YOU DID.

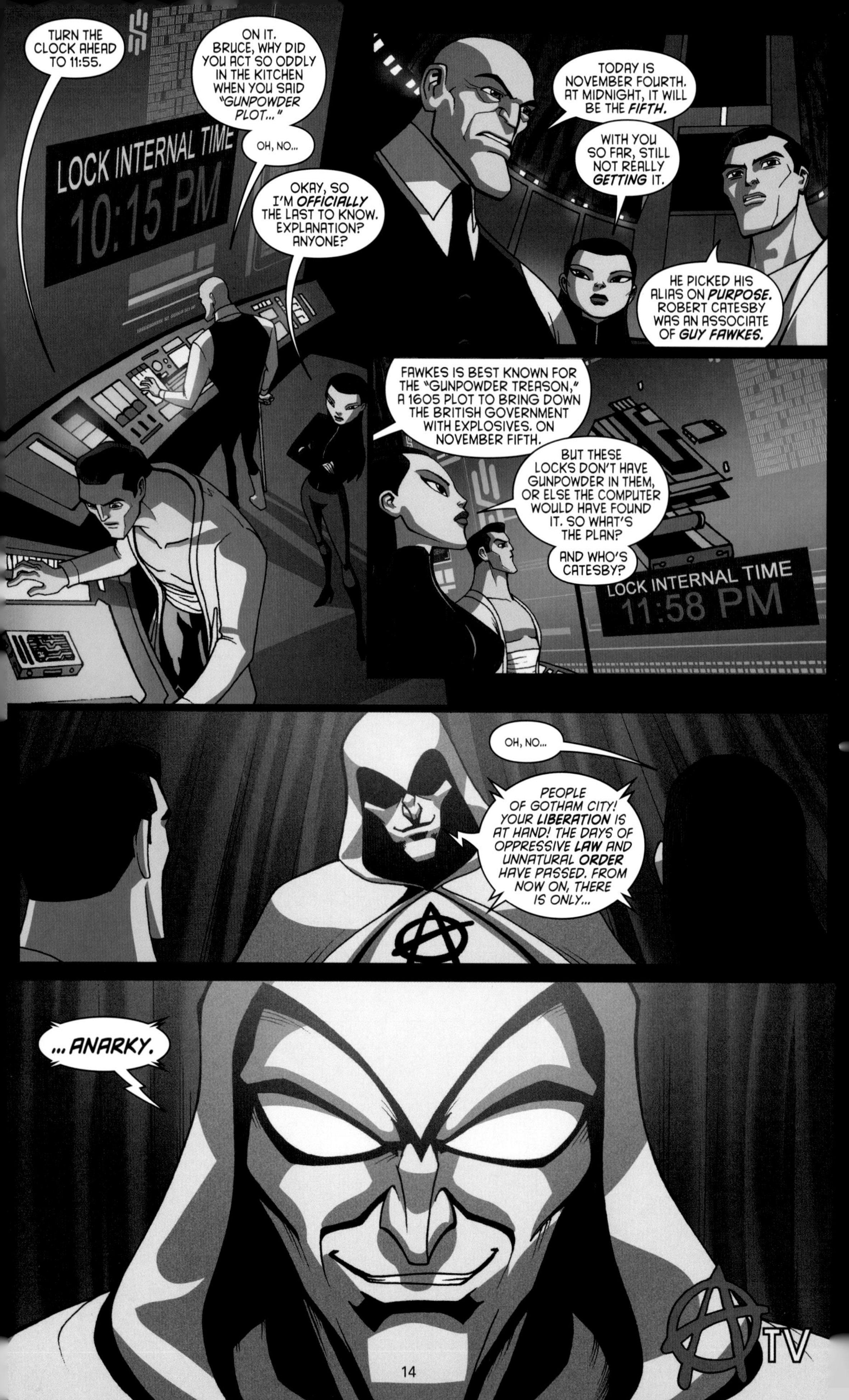
TURN THE CLOCK AHEAD TO 11:55.
LOCK INTERNAL TIME 10:15 PM
ON IT. BRUCE, WHY DID YOU ACT SO ODDLY IN THE KITCHEN WHEN YOU SAID "GUNPOWDER PLOT..."
OH, NO...
OKAY, SO I'M OFFICIALLY THE LAST TO KNOW. EXPLANATION? ANYONE?
TODAY IS NOVEMBER FOURTH. AT MIDNIGHT, IT WILL BE THE FIFTH.
WITH YOU SO FAR, STILL NOT REALLY GETTING IT.
HE PICKED HIS ALIAS ON PURPOSE. ROBERT CATESBY WAS AN ASSOCIATE OF GUY FAWKES.
FAWKES IS BEST KNOWN FOR THE "GUNPOWDER TREASON," A 1605 PLOT TO BRING DOWN THE BRITISH GOVERNMENT WITH EXPLOSIVES. ON NOVEMBER FIFTH.
BUT THESE LOCKS DON'T HAVE GUNPOWDER IN THEM, OR ELSE THE COMPUTER WOULD HAVE FOUND IT. SO WHAT'S THE PLAN?
AND WHO'S CATESBY?
LOCK INTERNAL TIME 11:58 PM
OH, NO...
PEOPLE OF GOTHAM CITY! YOUR LIBERATION IS AT HAND! THE DAYS OF OPPRESSIVE LAW AND UNNATURAL ORDER HAVE PASSED. FROM NOW ON, THERE IS ONLY...
...ANARKY.
TV

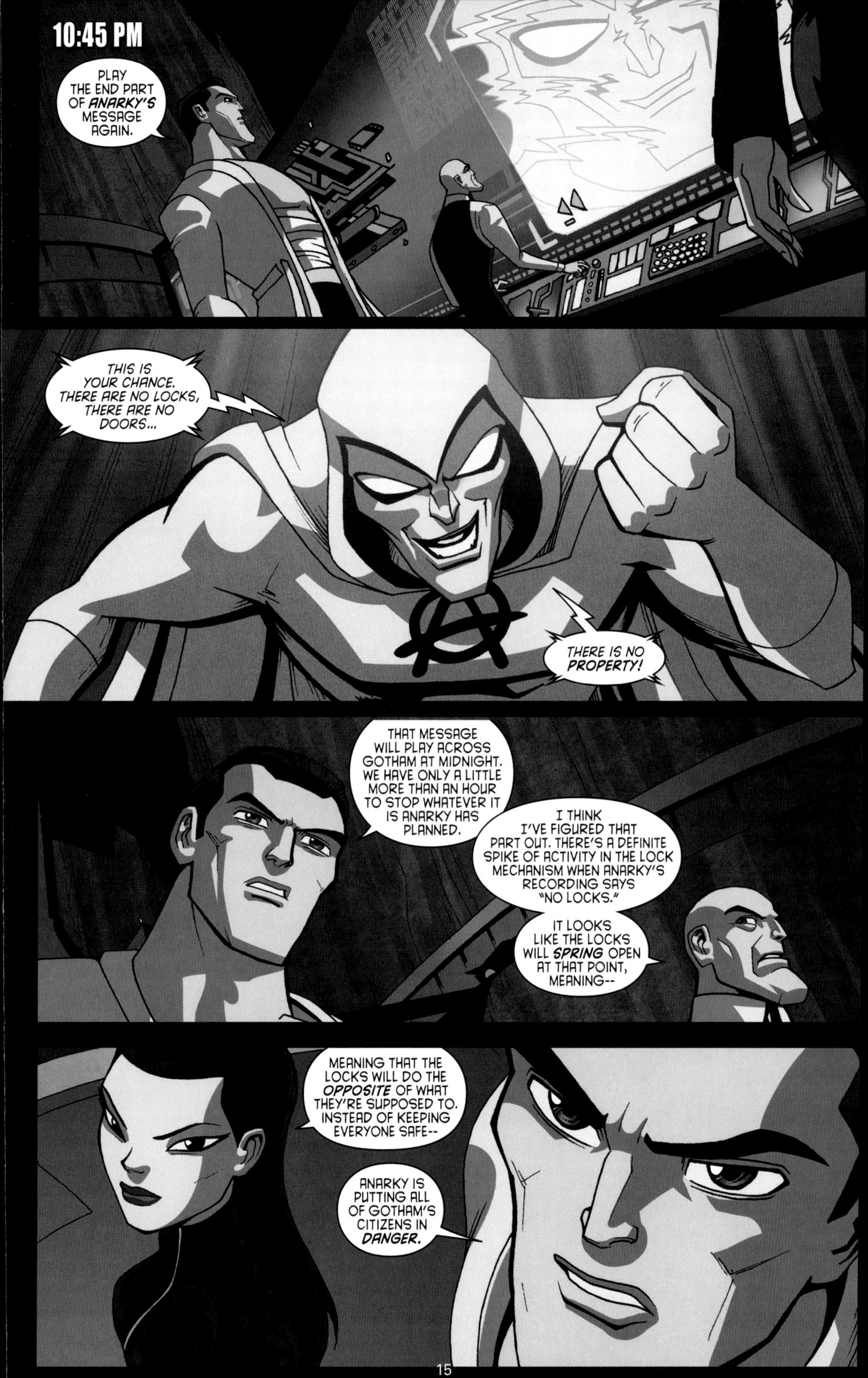
10:45 PM
PLAY THE END PART OF ANARKY'S MESSAGE AGAIN.
THIS IS YOUR CHANCE. THERE ARE NO LOCKS, THERE ARE NO DOORS...
THERE IS NO PROPERTY!
THAT MESSAGE WILL PLAY ACROSS GOTHAM AT MIDNIGHT. WE HAVE ONLY A LITTLE MORE THAN AN HOUR TO STOP WHATEVER IT IS ANARKY HAS PLANNED.
I THINK I'VE FIGURED THAT PART OUT. THERE'S A DEFINITE SPIKE OF ACTIVITY IN THE LOCK MECHANISM WHEN ANARKY'S RECORDING SAYS "NO LOCKS."
IT LOOKS LIKE THE LOCKS WILL SPRING OPEN AT THAT POINT, MEANING--
MEANING THAT THE LOCKS WILL DO THE OPPOSITE OF WHAT THEY'RE SUPPOSED TO. INSTEAD OF KEEPING EVERYONE SAFE--
ANARKY IS PUTTING ALL OF GOTHAM'S CITIZENS IN DANGER.

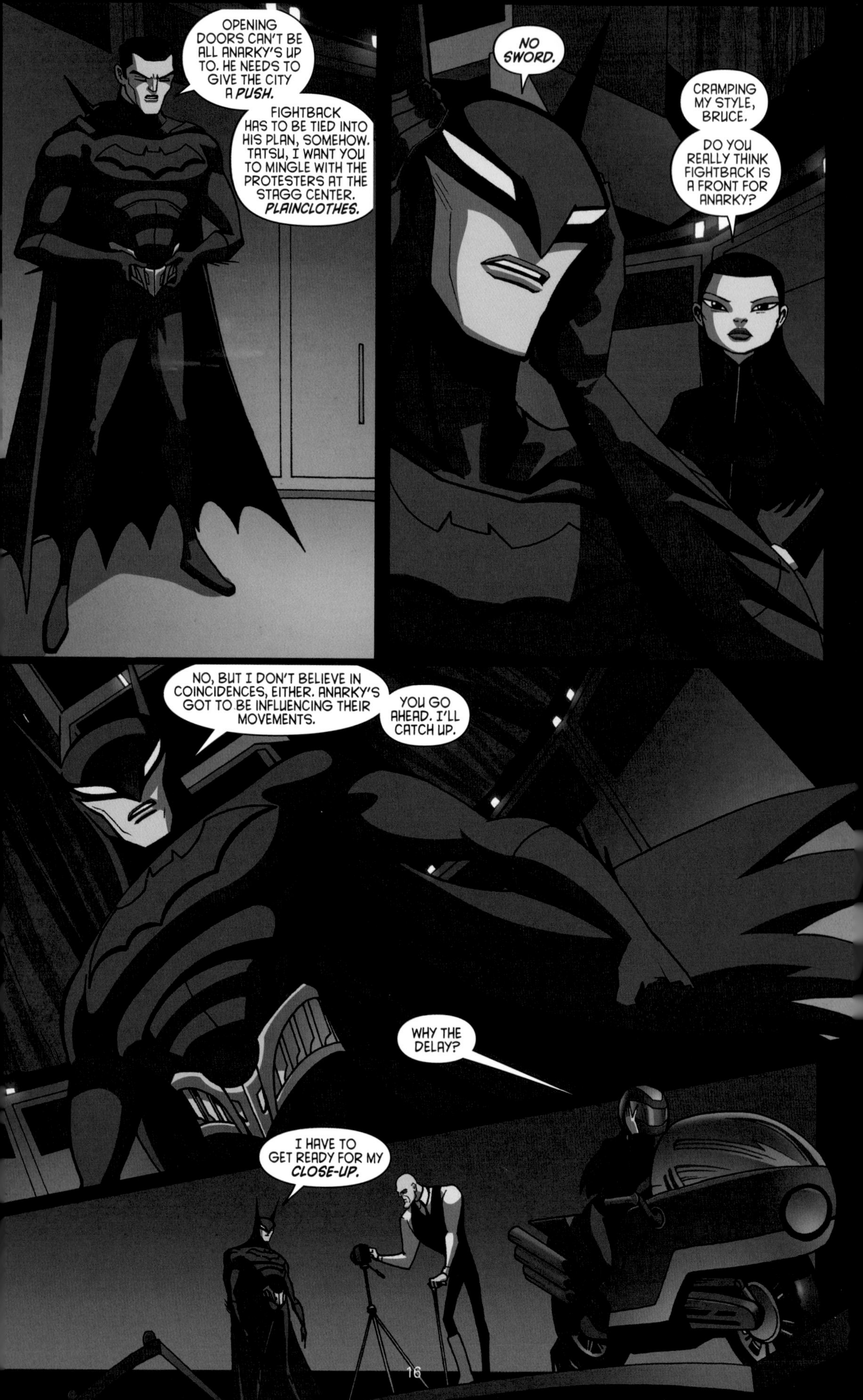

OPENING DOORS CAN'T BE ALL ANARKY'S UP TO. HE NEEDS TO GIVE THE CITY A *PUSH.*
FIGHTBACK HAS TO BE TIED INTO HIS PLAN, SOMEHOW. TATSU, I WANT YOU TO MINGLE WITH THE PROTESTERS AT THE STAGG CENTER. ***PLAINCLOTHES.***
NO SWORD.
CRAMPING MY STYLE, BRUCE.
DO YOU REALLY THINK FIGHTBACK IS A FRONT FOR ANARKY?
NO, BUT I DON'T BELIEVE IN COINCIDENCES, EITHER. ANARKY'S GOT TO BE INFLUENCING THEIR MOVEMENTS.
YOU GO AHEAD. I'LL CATCH UP.
WHY THE DELAY?
I HAVE TO GET READY FOR MY ***CLOSE-UP.***

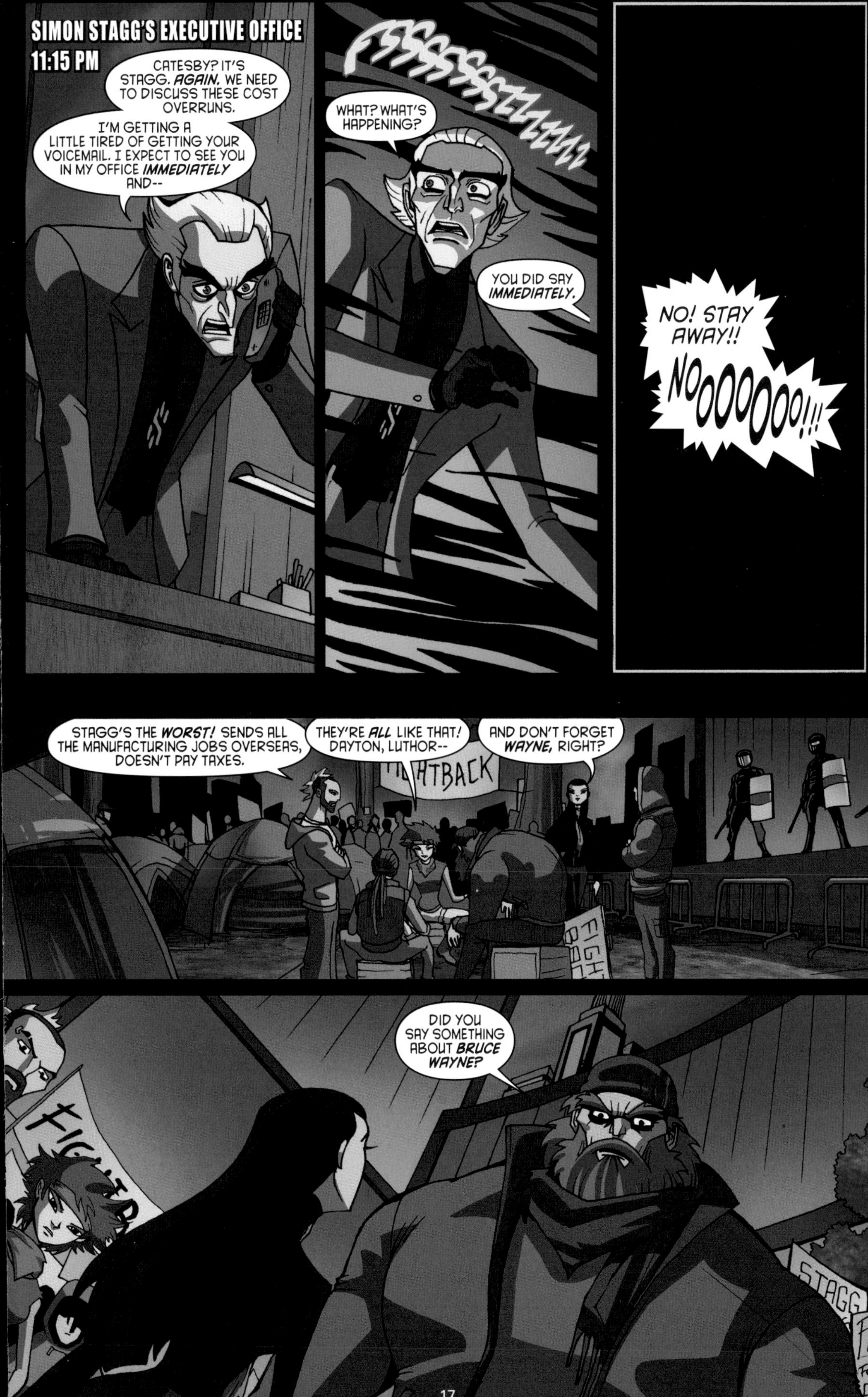
SIMON STAGG'S EXECUTIVE OFFICE
11:15 PM
CATESBY? IT'S STAGG. AGAIN. WE NEED TO DISCUSS THESE COST OVERRUNS.
I'M GETTING A LITTLE TIRED OF GETTING YOUR VOICEMAIL. I EXPECT TO SEE YOU IN MY OFFICE IMMEDIATELY AND--
FSSSSSSSZZZZZZZ
WHAT? WHAT'S HAPPENING?
YOU DID SAY IMMEDIATELY.
NO! STAY AWAY!!
NOOOOOOO!!!
STAGG'S THE WORST! SENDS ALL THE MANUFACTURING JOBS OVERSEAS, DOESN'T PAY TAXES.
THEY'RE ALL LIKE THAT! DAYTON, LUTHOR--
AND DON'T FORGET WAYNE, RIGHT?
DID YOU SAY SOMETHING ABOUT BRUCE WAYNE?

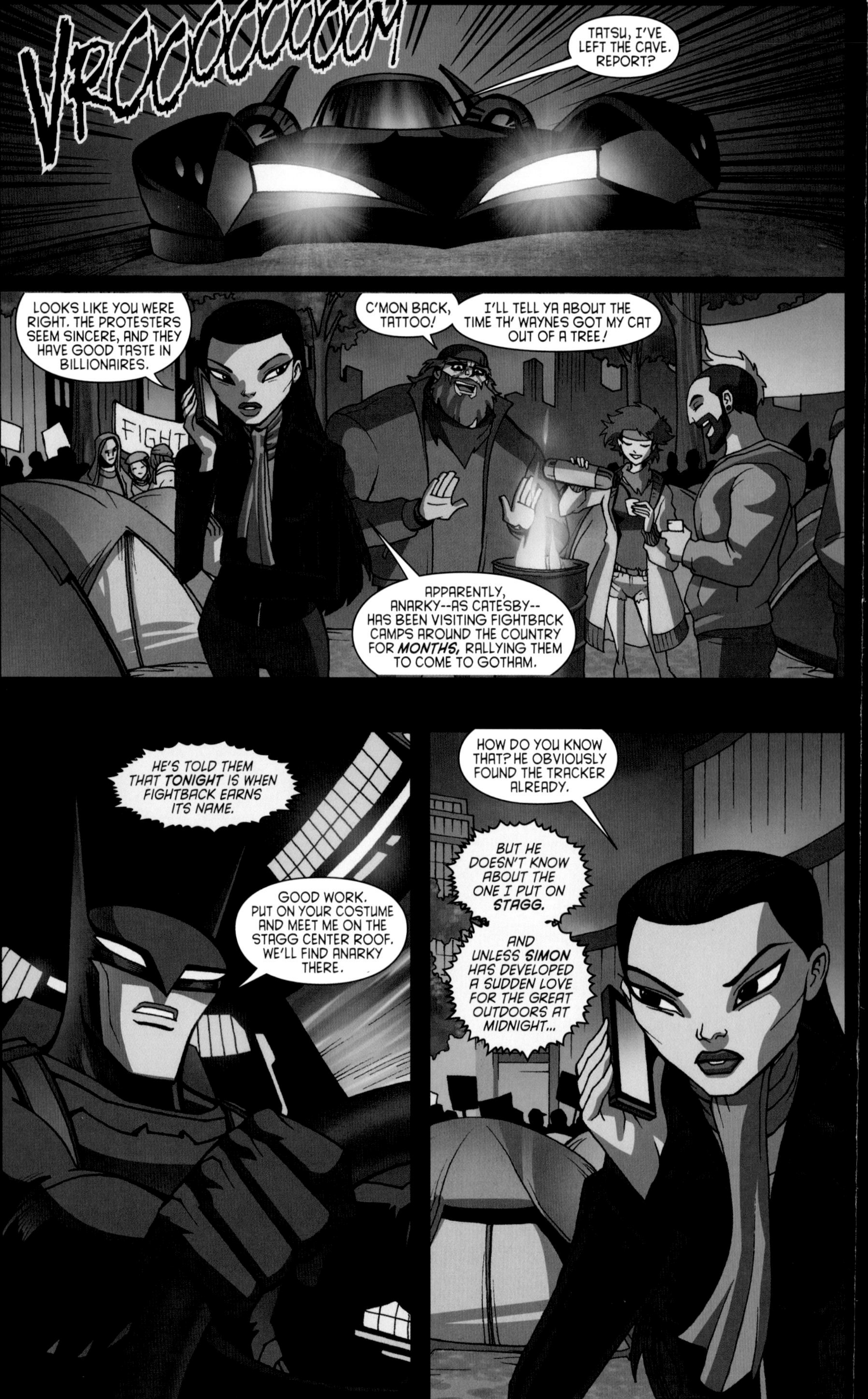
VROOOOOOOOOM
TATSU, I'VE LEFT THE CAVE. REPORT?
LOOKS LIKE YOU WERE RIGHT. THE PROTESTERS SEEM SINCERE, AND THEY HAVE GOOD TASTE IN BILLIONAIRES.
FIGHT
C'MON BACK, TATTOO!
I'LL TELL YA ABOUT THE TIME TH' WAYNES GOT MY CAT OUT OF A TREE!
APPARENTLY, ANARKY--AS CATESBY--HAS BEEN VISITING FIGHTBACK CAMPS AROUND THE COUNTRY FOR MONTHS, RALLYING THEM TO COME TO GOTHAM.
HE'S TOLD THEM THAT TONIGHT IS WHEN FIGHTBACK EARNS ITS NAME.
GOOD WORK. PUT ON YOUR COSTUME AND MEET ME ON THE STAGG CENTER ROOF. WE'LL FIND ANARKY THERE.
HOW DO YOU KNOW THAT? HE OBVIOUSLY FOUND THE TRACKER ALREADY.
BUT HE DOESN'T KNOW ABOUT THE ONE I PUT ON STAGG.
AND UNLESS SIMON HAS DEVELOPED A SUDDEN LOVE FOR THE GREAT OUTDOORS AT MIDNIGHT...

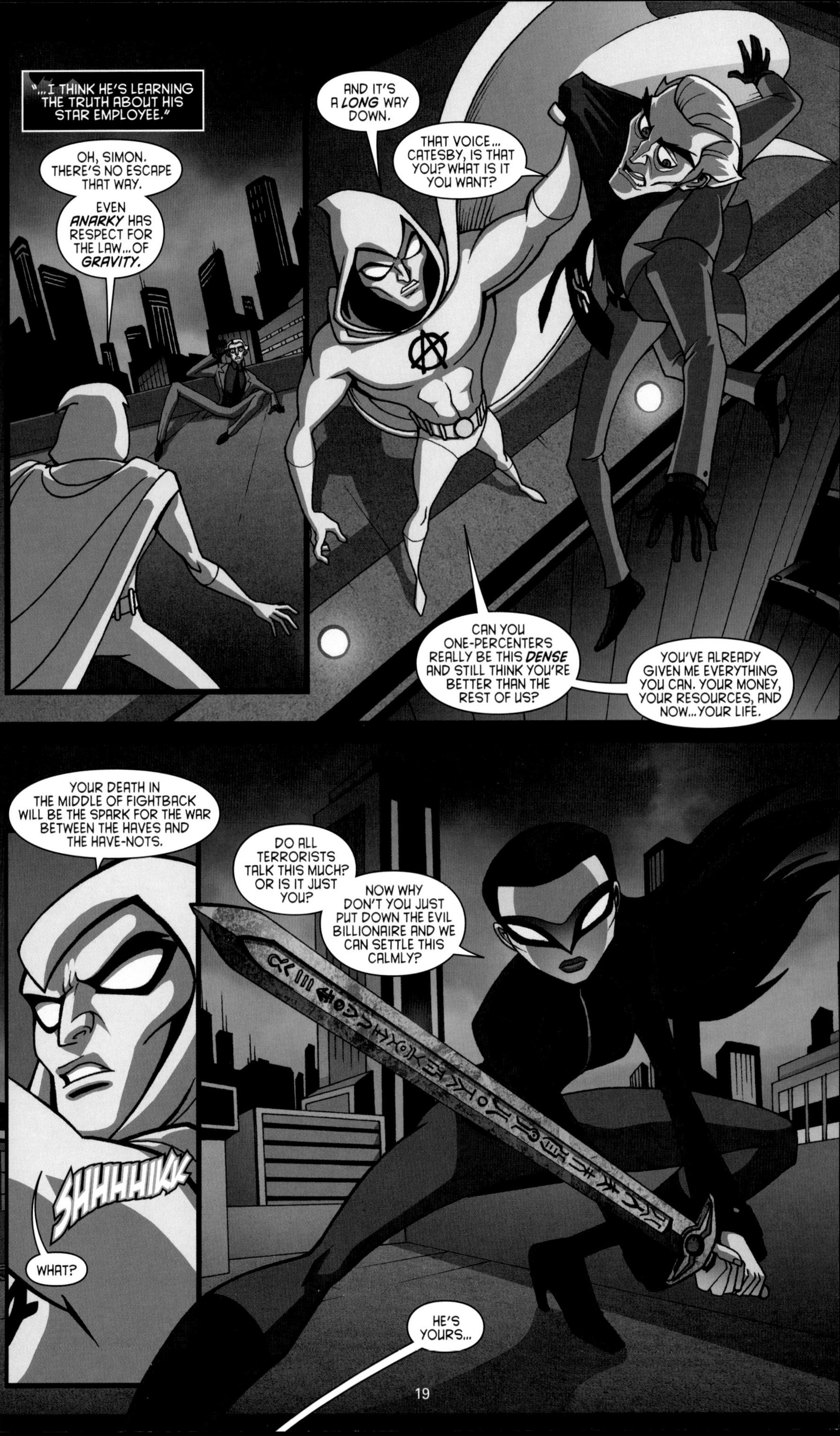
"...I THINK HE'S LEARNING THE TRUTH ABOUT HIS STAR EMPLOYEE."
OH, SIMON. THERE'S NO ESCAPE THAT WAY.
EVEN ANARKY HAS RESPECT FOR THE LAW...OF GRAVITY.
AND IT'S A LONG WAY DOWN.
THAT VOICE... CATESBY, IS THAT YOU? WHAT IS IT YOU WANT?
CAN YOU ONE-PERCENTERS REALLY BE THIS DENSE AND STILL THINK YOU'RE BETTER THAN THE REST OF US?
YOU'VE ALREADY GIVEN ME EVERYTHING YOU CAN. YOUR MONEY, YOUR RESOURCES, AND NOW...YOUR LIFE.
YOUR DEATH IN THE MIDDLE OF FIGHTBACK WILL BE THE SPARK FOR THE WAR BETWEEN THE HAVES AND THE HAVE-NOTS.
DO ALL TERRORISTS TALK THIS MUCH? OR IS IT JUST YOU?
NOW WHY DON'T YOU JUST PUT DOWN THE EVIL BILLIONAIRE AND WE CAN SETTLE THIS CALMLY?
SHHHHIKK
WHAT?
HE'S YOURS...

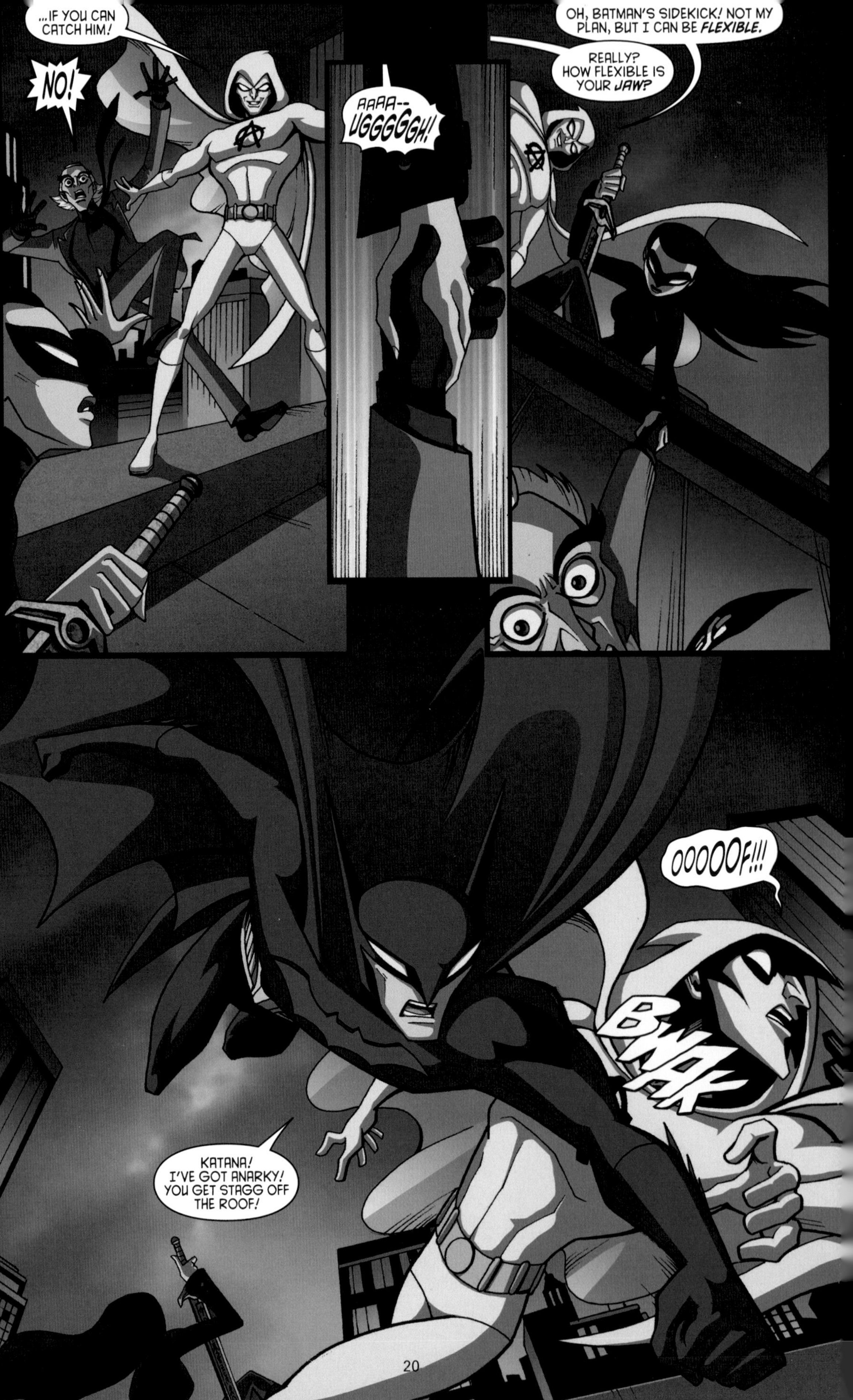
...IF YOU CAN CATCH HIM!
NO!
AAAA-- UGGGGGH!
OH, BATMAN'S SIDEKICK! NOT MY PLAN, BUT I CAN BE *FLEXIBLE.*
REALLY? HOW FLEXIBLE IS YOUR *JAW?*
OOOOOF!!!
BWAK
KATANA! I'VE GOT ANARKY! YOU GET STAGG OFF THE ROOF!

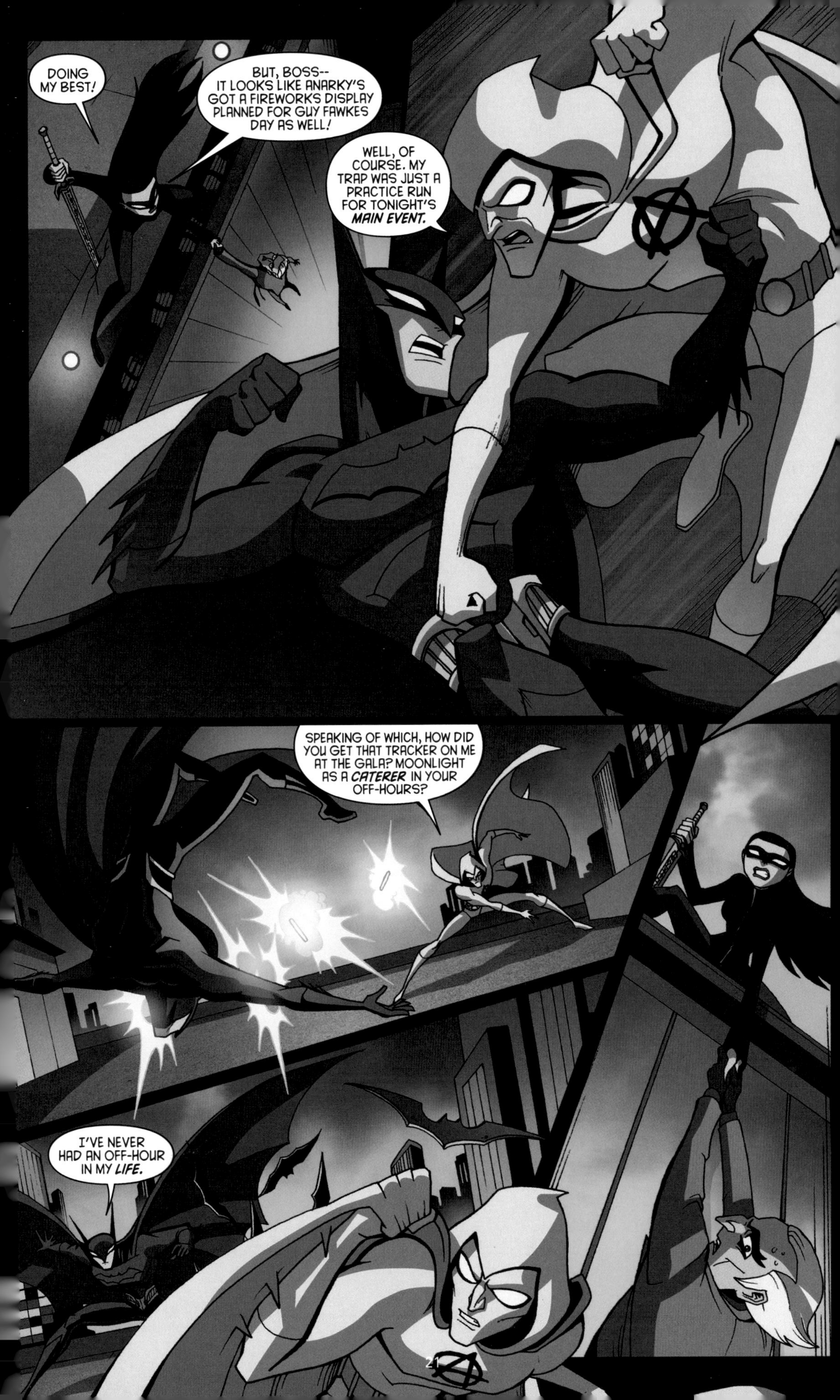
DOING MY BEST!
BUT, BOSS-- IT LOOKS LIKE ANARKY'S GOT A FIREWORKS DISPLAY PLANNED FOR GUY FAWKES DAY AS WELL!
WELL, OF COURSE. MY TRAP WAS JUST A PRACTICE RUN FOR TONIGHT'S *MAIN EVENT.*
SPEAKING OF WHICH, HOW DID YOU GET THAT TRACKER ON ME AT THE GALA? MOONLIGHT AS A *CATERER* IN YOUR OFF-HOURS?
I'VE NEVER HAD AN OFF-HOUR IN MY *LIFE.*

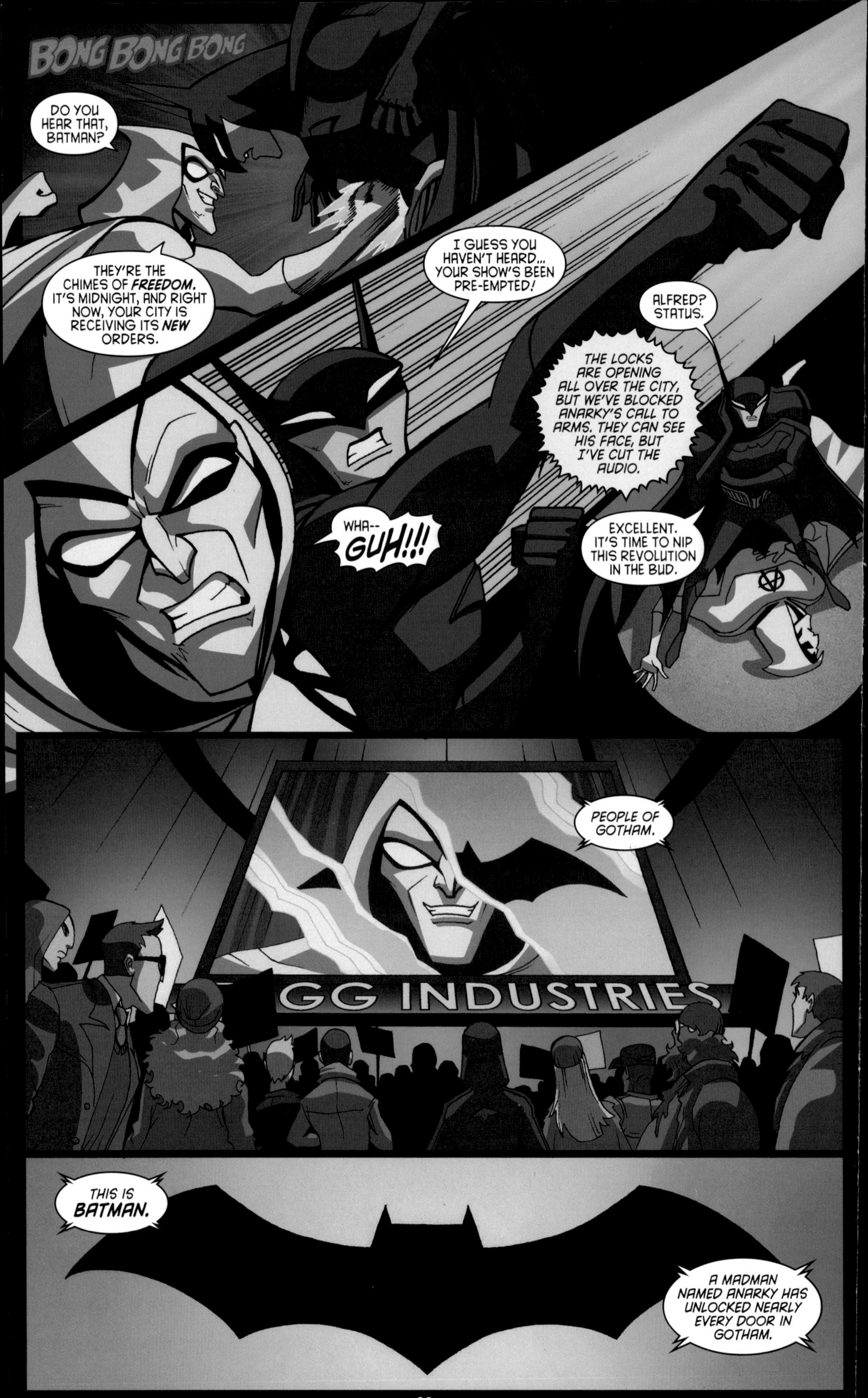
BONG BONG BONG
DO YOU HEAR THAT, BATMAN?
THEY'RE THE CHIMES OF FREEDOM. IT'S MIDNIGHT, AND RIGHT NOW, YOUR CITY IS RECEIVING ITS NEW ORDERS.
I GUESS YOU HAVEN'T HEARD... YOUR SHOW'S BEEN PRE-EMPTED!
WHA-- GUH!!!
ALFRED? STATUS.
THE LOCKS ARE OPENING ALL OVER THE CITY, BUT WE'VE BLOCKED ANARKY'S CALL TO ARMS. THEY CAN SEE HIS FACE, BUT I'VE CUT THE AUDIO.
EXCELLENT. IT'S TIME TO NIP THIS REVOLUTION IN THE BUD.
PEOPLE OF GOTHAM.
GG INDUSTRIES
THIS IS BATMAN.
A MADMAN NAMED ANARKY HAS UNLOCKED NEARLY EVERY DOOR IN GOTHAM.

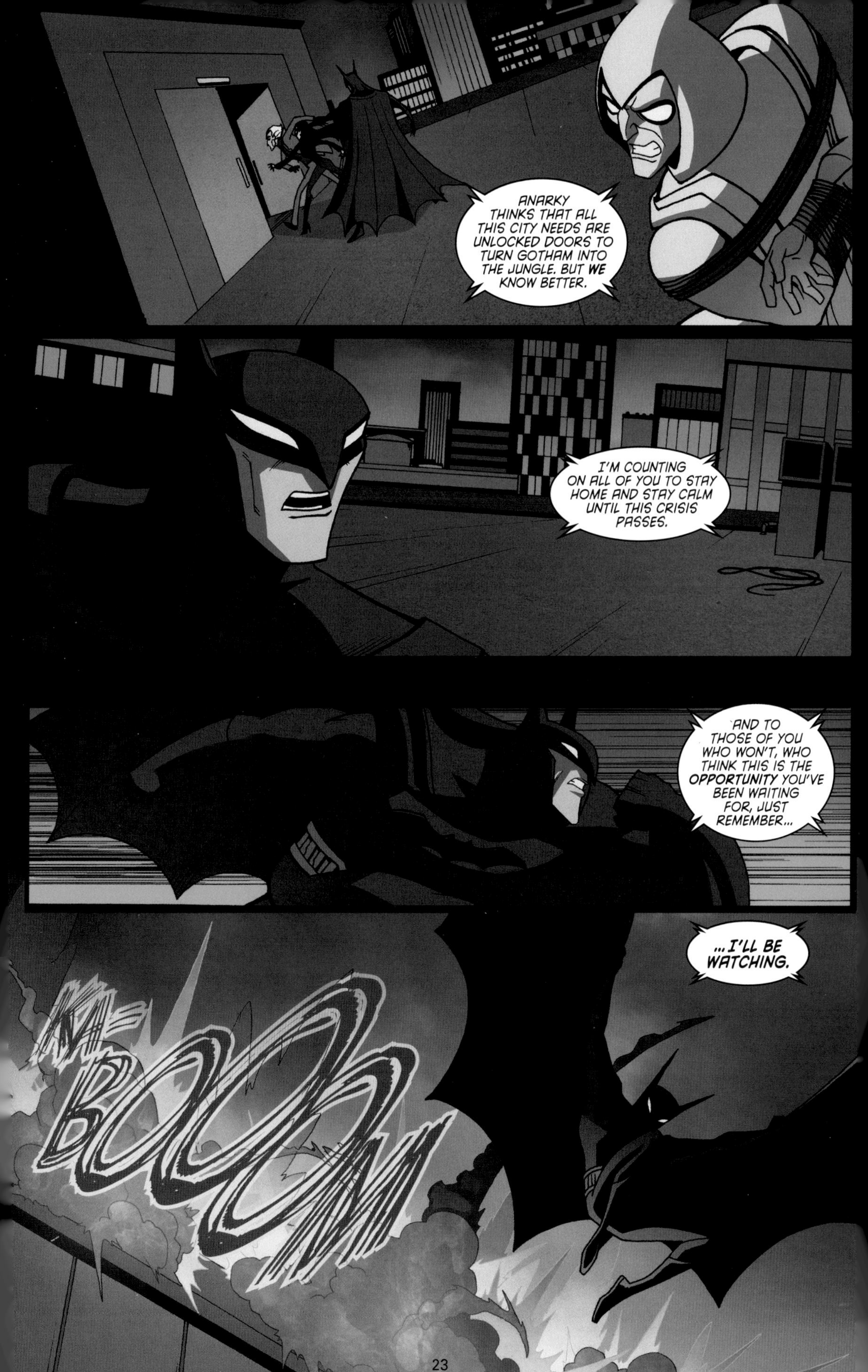
ANARKY THINKS THAT ALL THIS CITY NEEDS ARE UNLOCKED DOORS TO TURN GOTHAM INTO THE JUNGLE. BUT **WE** KNOW BETTER.
I'M COUNTING ON ALL OF YOU TO STAY HOME AND STAY CALM UNTIL THIS CRISIS PASSES.
AND TO THOSE OF YOU WHO WON'T, WHO THINK THIS IS THE **OPPORTUNITY** YOU'VE BEEN WAITING FOR, JUST REMEMBER...
...I'LL BE WATCHING.

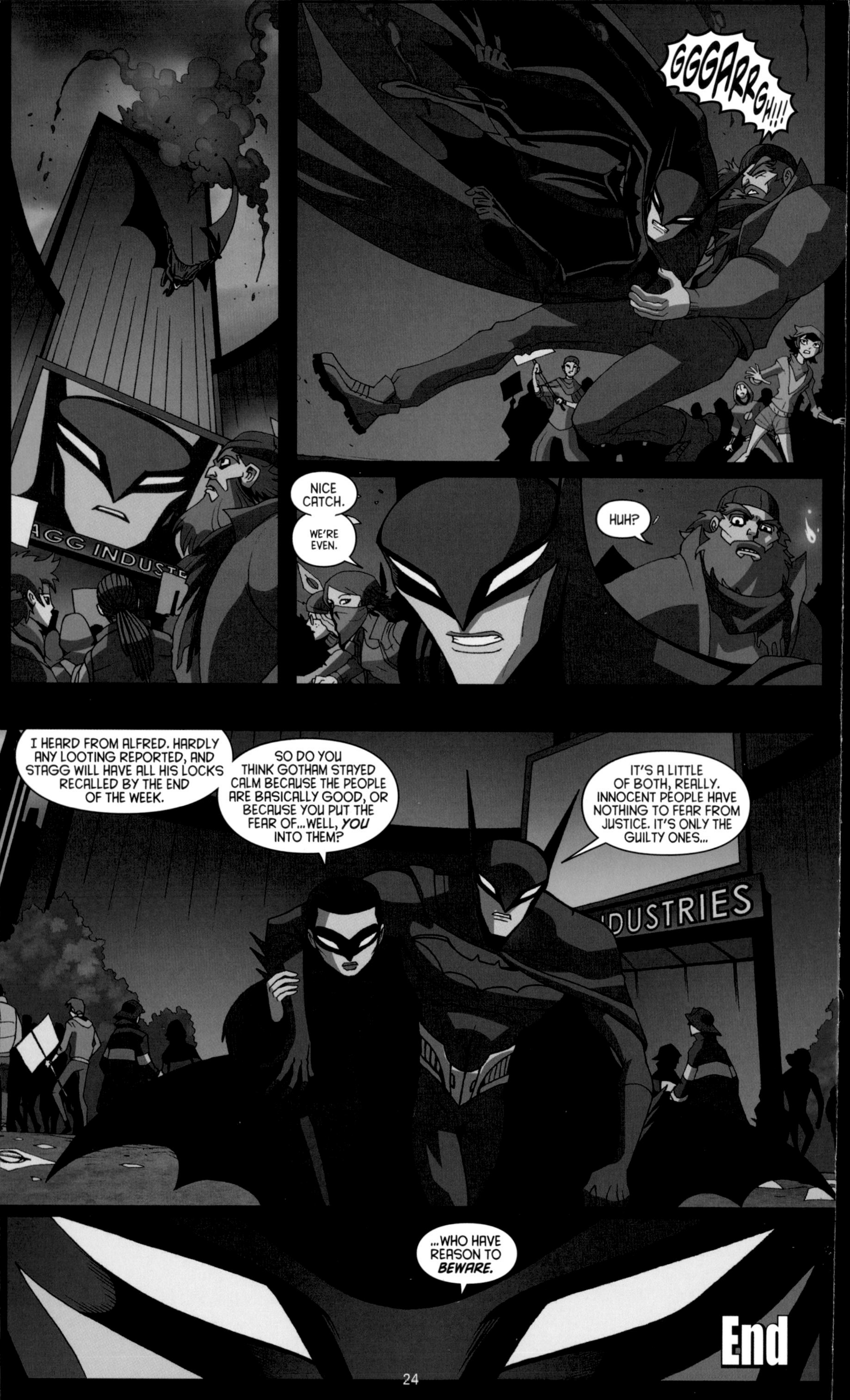
GGGARRGH!!!
NICE CATCH.
WE'RE EVEN.
HUH?
I HEARD FROM ALFRED. HARDLY ANY LOOTING REPORTED, AND STAGG WILL HAVE ALL HIS LOCKS RECALLED BY THE END OF THE WEEK.
SO DO YOU THINK GOTHAM STAYED CALM BECAUSE THE PEOPLE ARE BASICALLY GOOD, OR BECAUSE YOU PUT THE FEAR OF...WELL, *YOU* INTO THEM?
IT'S A LITTLE OF BOTH, REALLY. INNOCENT PEOPLE HAVE NOTHING TO FEAR FROM JUSTICE. IT'S ONLY THE GUILTY ONES...
...WHO HAVE REASON TO *BEWARE.*
End

CREATORS

IVAN COHEN — WRITER

A former editor and media-development executive at DC Comics, Ivan Cohen worked on the DC Universe line of direct-to-video animated movies as well as the popular TV series *Smallville, Batman: The Brave and the Bold*, and *Young Justice*. As a writer, Cohen's recent credits include the *Green Lantern: The Animated Series* comic book, articles for *Time Out* magazine, and an episode of the upcoming Cartoon Network television series *Beware The Batman*. The co-producer of *Secret Origin: The Story of DC Comics* [2010], he is a consultant on the upcoming PBS documentary Superheroes: *The Never-Ending Battle*.

LUCIANO VECCHIO — ILLUSTRATOR

Luciano Vecchio currently lives in Buenos Aires, Argentina. With experience in illustration, animation, and comics, his works have been published in the US, Spain, the UK, France, and Argentina. His credits include Ben 10 [DC Comics], Cruel Thing [Norma], Unseen Tribe [Zuda Comics], Sentinels [Drumfish Productions], and several DC Super Heroes books for Stone Arch Books.

GLOSSARY

alias [A·lee·uhss]--used to indicate an additional name that a person (such as a criminal) sometimes uses

crisis [CRY·sis]--a difficult or dangerous situation that needs serious attention

embedded [em·BED·id]--placed or set something in something else

encounter [en·KOWN·ter]--to have or experience something, or to meet someone without expecting or intending to

false face [FAHLSS FAYSS]--a mask covering the face

foreman [FORE·man]--a person who is in charge of a group of workers

forensics [fuh·REN·ziks]--the study or science of solving crimes by using scientific knowledge or methods

mingle [MING·guhl]--to move around during a party, meeting, etc., and talk informally with different people

ruffians [RUFF·ee·uhnz]--strong and violent people who threaten and hurt other people

treason [TREE·zuhn]--the crime of trying to overthrow your country's government or of helping your country's enemies during war

yields [YEELDZ]--produces or provides something

VISUAL QUESTIONS & PROMPTS

1. Why are Anarky's speech bubbles jagged? Reread pages 14-15 for clues.

THIS IS YOUR CHANCE. THERE ARE NO LOCKS, THERE ARE NO DOORS...
THERE IS NO PROPERTY!
1

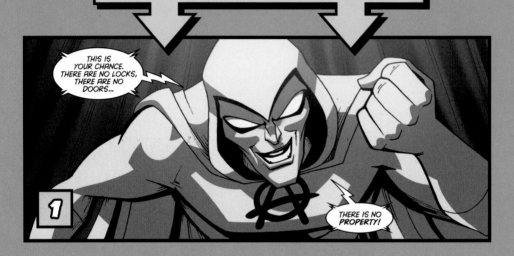

2. Why did the artists choose to show Batman's eyes up close in this panel? How does it make you feel?

2

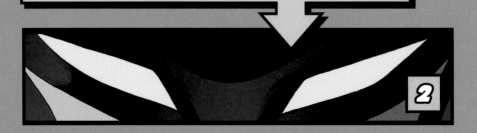

3. Batman has a variety of skills he uses to fight crime. Which of his many skills were the most helpful in stopping Anarky's plot? His detective skills? His fighting ability? Something else?

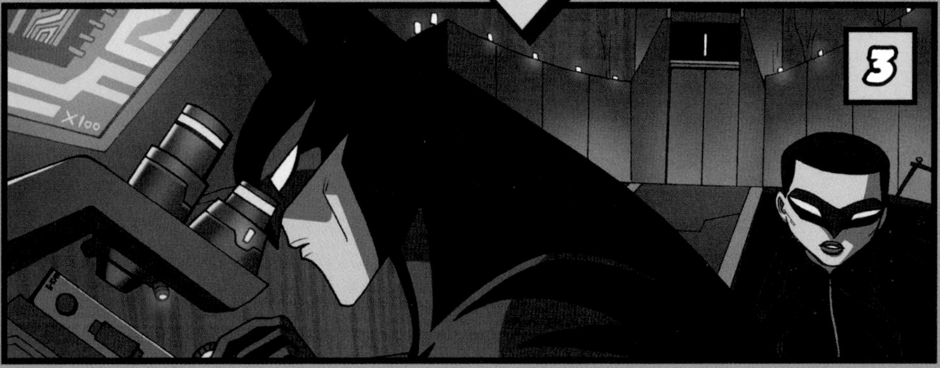
3
X100

4. What does Batman mean when he tells the protester that they are even? If you aren't sure, reread the panels that the bearded character appears in earlier in the book.

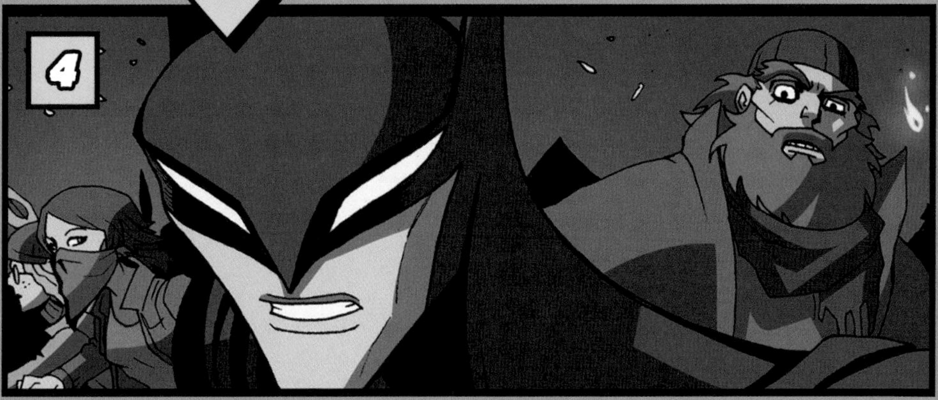
4

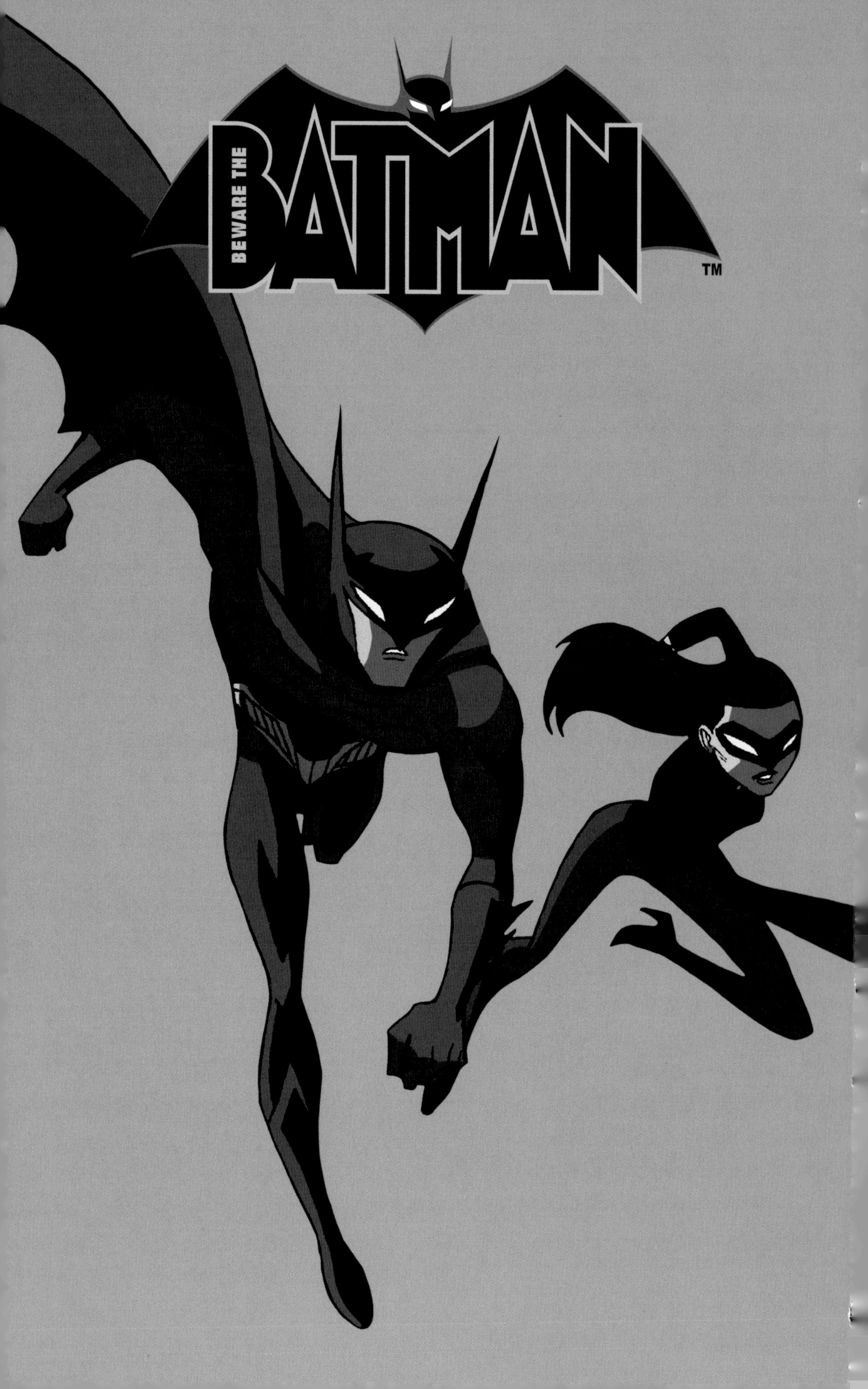
BEWARE THE
BATMAN™

READ THEM ALL!

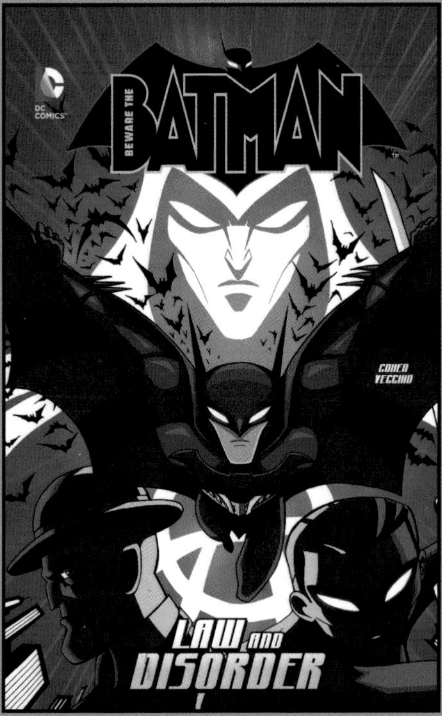
DC COMICS
BEWARE THE BATMAN
COHEN
VECCHIO
LAW AND DISORDER

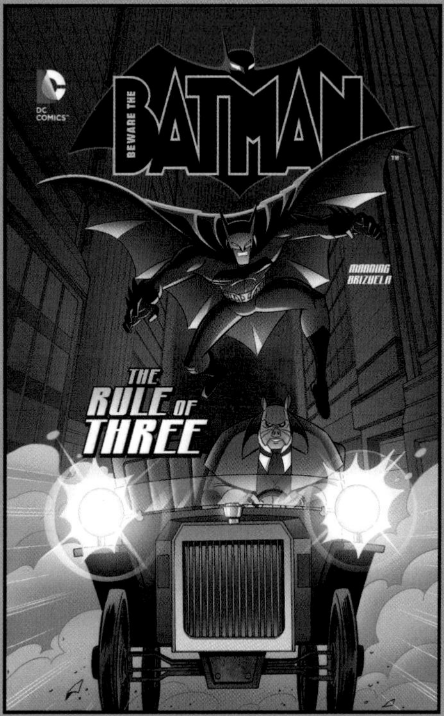
DC COMICS
BEWARE THE BATMAN
MANNING
BRIZUELA
THE RULE OF THREE

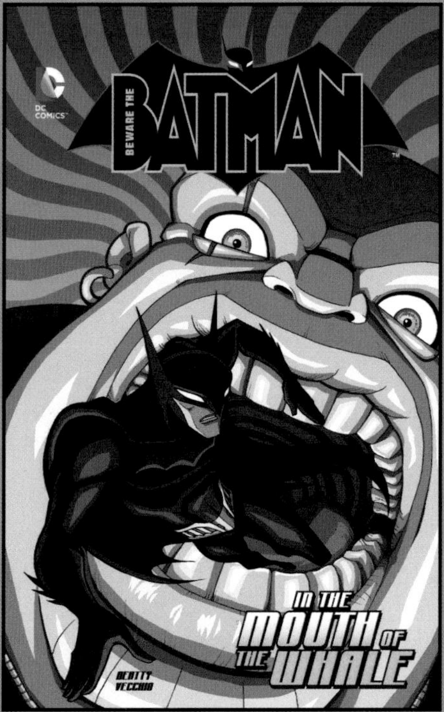
DC COMICS
BEWARE THE BATMAN
IN THE MOUTH OF THE WHALE
BEATTY
VECCHIO

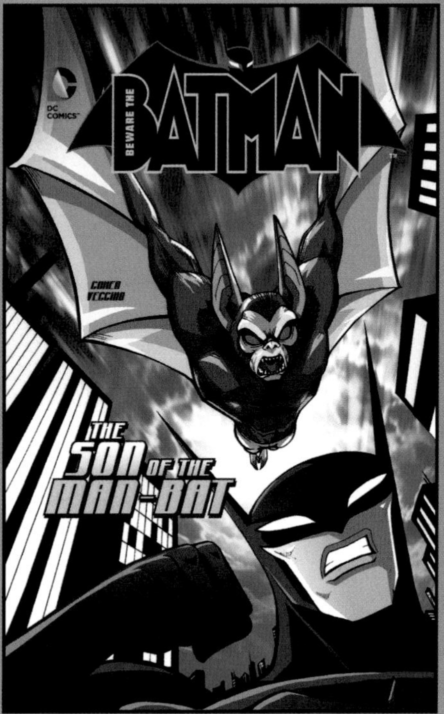
DC COMICS
BEWARE THE BATMAN
COHEN
VECCHIO
THE SON OF THE MAN-BAT

BEWARE THE BATMAN™

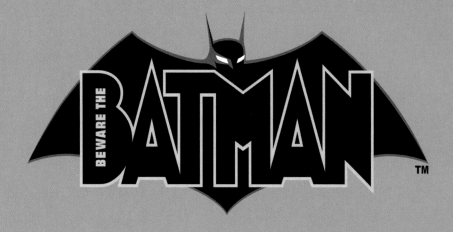